UNWAVERING SECURITY

SALTWATER COWBOYS, BOOK 6

CHRISTY BARRITT

River Heights

COMPLETE BOOK LIST

For a complete list of books by Christy Barritt, please visit her website.

CHAPTER ONE

MIRANDA STEWART PULLED her flannel shirt tighter around her shoulders as a cool wind swept across the island. She glanced around, looking for a sign someone was following her.

She didn't see anyone or anything other than the dark clouds in the distance—clouds that crept closer and closer.

But that didn't mean she was out here alone.

Maybe going on a walk by herself had been a bad idea. But the urge to flee Abigail Ferguson's house had overwhelmed her.

Abigail had told her that Thaddeus Blackwell was set to arrive from Texas anytime now.

She didn't want to face that man again.

Miranda knew she'd eventually have to see

Thaddeus since he was the best man and Miranda was the maid of honor in their best friends' wedding. She thought she'd prepared herself for this reunion, that she'd cast aside her hurt at his rejection and was ready to keep her chin up.

But now that the moment was upon her, she knew she hadn't.

Miranda paused at the edge of the road and looked around. She must have walked a mile already —a mile filled with weather-worn beach houses, wild horses, and sandy roads.

Yes, sandy roads.

Abigail's fiancé, Grant Matthews, had told her all about the island on the drive and boat ride over to Cape Corral, North Carolina. The community had no paved roads because of the shifting nature of the sand. In fact, the only bridge leading to the island had been washed out in a storm and was still being rebuilt.

This trip had already been quite the adventure.

And she'd just arrived from New York last night.

What if danger had followed her here?

Someone had been leaving disturbing notes for her. On more than one occasion, she'd felt unseen eyes watching her. Then there were her ex-boyfriend's words to her after Miranda had told him she didn't want to see him anymore.

I'll do whatever it takes to get you back.

The words had haunted Miranda ever since.

For some people, his statement might have sounded sweet. But coming from Brian Bowers, the words sounded ominous to her.

The two of them had only dated for about five months, but it was long enough to know something wasn't right with him. Really, Miranda had only dated Brian because she'd been trying to push Thaddeus out of her mind by dating someone else. Brian hadn't measured up to Thaddeus, however.

She had a feeling no one ever would.

But that didn't matter because Thaddeus clearly hadn't returned her feelings.

She took another step, determined to walk a little farther and collect her thoughts.

At the idea of seeing Thaddeus again, insecurities roared to life. Suddenly all the accomplishments Miranda had worked so hard to achieve disappeared from her mind. She was back to being the gawky girl with the awkward social interactions. The girl who loved all things sci-fi and fantasy. Whose one wish after high school graduation had been visiting The

Wizarding World of Harry Potter at Universal Studios.

All those years of being an ugly duckling still played with her psyche sometimes—and once her self-doubt set in, the feelings were hard to shake.

"You need to get over it, Miranda," she mumbled to herself. "No man is worth this kind of agony."

Despite the mild October day, Miranda shivered again. If it wasn't for the fact she loved Abigail so much, Miranda wouldn't have come here at all. But she wasn't that kind of friend, and she certainly wasn't going to let Thaddeus stop her from supporting her bestie on Abigail's big day—even if the man had broken her heart.

As she continued walking, a huge sand dune rose in the distance, much bigger than those along the shoreline. The climb definitely looked challenging.

She stared at it a moment before shrugging. "Why not?"

She'd soak in the view at the top. Then she'd head back.

She couldn't avoid Thaddeus forever. She needed to both face him and maintain her dignity.

But maybe she could buy herself a little more time and compose what she was going to say to the handsome, Texas-born FBI agent.

Thanks for the wonderful evening eight months ago. I thought we had something special, but, apparently, I was wrong. I never heard from you again.

I've never been kissed like you kissed me. But I guess I was just any other girl to you.

An utterly forgettable girl.

More tension grew inside her, her burning calves the only thing grounding her as she neared the crest of the dune.

Goosebumps suddenly rose across her skin.

There it was again. That feeling. The sense that unseen eyes were on her.

As she glanced around the other side of the dune, she spotted a shadow by a cluster of trees near the base of the dune.

She blinked.

Then nothing.

Had someone been there? Or was she seeing things? For all she knew, the movement could be one of the wild horses lingering in the brush.

Still, her senses heightened.

Being out here alone hadn't been a good idea. She should turn around and head back to Abigail's.

She paused again, glancing at that cluster of trees for a sign of any movement.

She saw nothing. She'd probably just been seeing things.

Quickly, she glanced to the other side, where the mighty Atlantic churned. The ocean was so beautiful. She'd be perfectly content to stay here all day and observe the waves racing forward only to run away again.

But not with a storm coming.

Not when someone could be watching her.

And not when she had maid of honor duties to perform.

As she turned to head back, Miranda sensed movement behind her—a subtle shift in the sand, the sound of heavy but muted footfalls.

Before she could turn, something hard rammed into the back of her head.

Then she collapsed into darkness.

———

THADDEUS BLACKWELL DREADED BEING around Miranda Stewart again.

Especially considering the way things had played out last time he'd seen her.

But Thaddeus was here for Grant, not for Miranda.

Certainly, the two of them could act like adults.

Grant walked with him to the front door of Abigail Ferguson's house. Before they even hit the top step, Abigail threw the door open.

"It's so good to see you again, Thaddeus." She pulled him into a warm hug. "It's been what? Seven or eight months?"

"Eight. Ever since the two of you came out to Texas to visit." And that's when Thaddeus' troubles had started.

That was when he'd met Miranda. She'd just happened to be in the area at the same time Abigail and Grant were, and the four of them had gone to dinner together.

They'd had an amazing time, and he'd shared a once-in-a-lifetime connection with Miranda.

Or at least he thought he had.

Turns out, none of it was real.

He frowned at the thought.

Speaking of which . . . he peered behind Abigail, looking for the woman. Grant had said Miranda was already here, that she'd arrived a few hours ago.

Thaddeus just needed to get this awkward reunion over and done with so he could move on.

Abigail seemed to read his mind. "Miranda took a walk. She should be back anytime now."

The warm tone with which Abigail said the words seemed to indicate that Miranda hadn't talked to her about the tense situation between the two of them.

So much had happened since that blind date. Dating anyone else had been the least of Thaddeus' concerns.

Especially after what happened with his partner.

But Thaddeus was determined to put all of that behind him.

"You know, actually, I'm getting a little worried." Abigail glanced at her watch. "I thought Miranda would be back by now. You guys didn't see her when you drove through town, did you?"

Grant shook his head. "I wasn't looking, but I would have probably seen her if she was walking down the main road. You don't think she got lost, do you?"

"She's always had a terrible sense of direction. I tried to call her phone a few minutes ago, and she didn't answer. That's what really concerns me." Abigail's frown deepened. "She usually answers her phone."

Thaddeus glanced at Grant and saw the worry on his face.

"Did she take her phone with her?" Thaddeus asked.

"I'm sure she did, but it's more than that," Abigail said. "I'm not sure what's going on with her, but something happened back in New York that has her spooked. She hasn't told me all the details. But she's seemed skittish ever since she got here. Between that and her sense of direction . . ."

"How about if the two of us go out and look for her?" Grant glanced at Thaddeus. "I know you just got here, but are you okay with that?"

If Grant and Abigail needed help, Thaddeus couldn't say no. "Of course. Why don't we split up so we can cover more ground?"

A few minutes later, Thaddeus was in Abigail's Jeep, heading toward the south side of the island while Grant took his truck north.

Thaddeus was probably the last person Miranda would want to see. But he really hoped her disappearance right now was all a misunderstanding and nothing more. On an island like this, how much trouble could she get into?

An image of Miranda flashed in his mind. Her honey-blonde hair. Warm brown eyes. Infectious laugh, goofy smile, and overall curious attitude.

His strong attraction to her had thrown him off

guard. Not because the woman wasn't attractive. She definitely was.

But because Thaddeus hadn't been looking to date anyone.

Miranda had been like a breath of fresh air with her down-to-earth attitude and easygoing personality. He felt like he could have stayed talking with her all night.

Then not long after, he'd discovered that none of it had been real. It was almost like he'd met two different people.

He frowned again.

A few minutes later, Thaddeus braked at the base of a huge sand dune.

There were no houses out here—just one gigantic mound of sand. How high was this dune? If he had to guess, probably eighty feet. It was probably as long as a football field, and maybe just as wide. Definitely a landmark to be explored by curious newcomers.

He parked the Jeep, minding the "No Motor Vehicles Allowed Beyond This Point" sign, and then climbed out, ready to search this area by foot.

As the wind picked up, Thaddeus knew the storm was getting closer and he'd soon be out of time. Plus, the sun should be setting in less than two hours, which would plunge the island into darkness. He'd noticed there were no streetlights here and only a smattering of homes.

Those things probably only added to this area's charm.

Unless you were lost out here in the dark.

He called Grant, wanting to make sure there were no updates before he ventured up the massive dune.

"Did you find her?" Grant skipped any formal greeting and got straight to the point.

"Not yet. I guess you haven't either?" He pushed his cowboy hat down harder on his head, worried the wind might carry it away.

"No, and she still isn't answering her phone. Let's hope we find her before the storm gets here. Forecasters are saying it could be pretty bad. Thunder, lightning, lots of rain, and high tides."

"I'll keep looking." As Thaddeus put his phone away, Miranda's image filled his mind again.

Miranda Stewart wasn't the kind of person he could easily forget.

In fact, he *hadn't* forgotten about her—even though he'd tried.

Nothing about the past eight months had turned out the way he'd thought it would. He'd simply accepted that life was what it was—full of disappointments, betrayals, and misjudgments.

As he continued climbing the dune, he saw someone near the other side of the massive sandpile.

It appeared to be a man.

Running away.

Toward a patch of woods in the distance.

Thaddeus' instincts went on alert.

What was that about?

He took a few more steps and crested the dune. As he did, he spotted something on the ground in the distance—a mix of flannel and jean shorts and skin.

Thaddeus quickened his steps.

As he got closer, a figure came into view.

A woman.

Was that . . . Miranda?

He took off in a jog, his cowboy boots digging into the sand.

Just as he reached the woman, he realized it *was* Miranda.

She lay unconscious in the sand . . . or was she dead?

CHAPTER TWO

"MIRANDA. MIRANDA!"

Someone shook her from her daze.

She tried to pull her eyes open. Tried to blink. To focus.

A blurry figure hovered above her.

A blurry figure wearing a cowboy hat.

"Are you okay?" a deep voice rushed.

Why did that rolling tone sound familiar?

Her thoughts swam, almost as if she were lost in a sea of . . . sand?

Nothing made sense.

Then she felt the ache. A throb pulsated in her head, each heartbeat sending waves of pain through her.

At once, she remembered someone sneaking up

behind her. Remembered feeling something smash into her head.

Miranda's lungs seized at the thought, and she drew back.

Was that same person in front of her now? The same one who'd knocked her out in the first place?

She had to get away.

Had to flee before he could hurt her any further.

"No, don't—" She tried to scoot away.

"Miranda, it's me. Thaddeus. Are you okay?"

Her stomach dropped as she realized why the voice sounded familiar.

Thaddeus? Was he really here right now?

One nightmare blurred into another.

As she blinked several more times, his face finally came into view.

He was just as handsome as she remembered. Dark hair with just a touch of curl, mesmerizing hazel eyes, a fit build.

He knelt beside her then helped her sit up.

Supported her as she collected herself.

Miranda should rebel against having his arms around her. She'd already made that mistake once when she'd allowed herself to get swept away with the moment, allowed herself to believe that Thaddeus could be the man of her dreams.

She'd been wrong.

But, right now, in this situation, she needed him.

There was no way she could make it back to Abigail's on her own.

"Miranda?"

Thaddeus was waiting for her response, she realized. Miranda pressed her eyes together as memories filled her.

"What happened?"

She rubbed the back of her head. "I was walking when someone came up behind me."

"Wait . . ." He squinted. "I saw someone running away from this area. Did he hurt you?"

"Yes, someone did." Miranda touched the back of her head again and felt a knot there. "But I didn't see who it was. He hit me with something, and everything went black, and now . . . here I am. With you. Wait. What *are* you doing out here?"

"Abigail was worried. I came looking for you." Thaddeus scowled and scanned their surroundings. "I don't like the sound of this. We should get you back and have you looked at."

"No. I'll be fine." She waved her hand in the air. "I don't want anything to take away from Abigail's wedding. Certainly not me getting hurt."

"You getting hurt would be an understatement. Someone assaulted you."

Miranda's stomach dropped again. Hearing the words out loud . . . it drove home just how serious this situation was.

Someone had wanted to harm her.

Brian?

Had he somehow followed her here? Would he take it that far?

Miranda wasn't sure. But the possibility made her want to fall apart. She needed time to absorb all that had happened. To sort things out in her mind.

As she tried to stand, Thaddeus quickly rose and helped her to her feet. He remained by her side as she took a few steps back and tried to find her balance. Instead, tension crept up her spine. What if the person who'd done this to her was still nearby? Still watching?

"Let's go back to Abigail's." Miranda swallowed hard as she stared up at Thaddeus. "Then we can figure things out. Please."

His jaw tightened as if he didn't like that idea. "Let me call Grant first and tell him I found you. Abigail has been worried sick."

"I didn't mean for any of this to happen."

Miranda ran a hand over her face, feeling like her day had gone from bad to worse.

"At least it's over now." Thaddeus reached for the phone in his pocket and paced beside her for a few steps.

Miranda wished she could believe his words. She had a sinking feeling this was far from over.

Before he could call Grant, the sand shifted beneath them.

Something cracked, splintered.

They suddenly dropped into darkness.

Then the sand swallowed them.

MIRANDA'S ARMS FLAILED.

She gasped, hardly able to comprehend what was happening.

Only that she was suspended in the air. That the breath had left her lungs. That her stomach plunged as if racing downhill on a roller-coaster.

Sand whooshed in her face, her eyes, her mouth as she continued to fall into the bottomless darkness.

She bounced off Thaddeus as he fell beside her. The impact jarring her bones.

Finally, she hit the ground with a thud.

She let out a moan and rubbed her backside before blinking, trying to get the grainy sand from her eyes.

Miranda turned and blinked several more times, desperate to soothe her irritated eyes. Finally, she spotted Thaddeus on the ground next to her.

A pinched expression twisted his face as he massaged his shoulder.

They'd fallen together through this trap door into the sandy dungeon below.

Fear shivered up her spine at the thought. "Are you okay?"

His features squeezed with discomfort as he rose to his feet. He grabbed his cowboy hat from the ground, let the sand fall off, and placed it on his head. "Been better. You?"

"Same."

He took her hand, his strong fingers closing over hers as he helped her to her feet. As he did, a zing raced through Miranda's blood.

The feeling was quickly overshadowed as an ache pulsated in her hip. She'd landed hard. But Miranda didn't think anything was broken, and that was the important thing.

She glanced up at what appeared to be a makeshift skylight.

But it wasn't. It was the area where she and Thaddeus had been standing only seconds earlier. The opening was at least ten feet from the floor, and a few broken pieces of wood edged the space.

"What in the world . . . ?" Thaddeus stared up.

"I'm not well versed on these types of things. But are we in a bunker of some sort?" Miranda inadvertently moved closer to the man, craving any type of security and familiarity she could find—even if it was of the heartbreaking variety.

"I don't know what this place is." Thaddeus continued to stare above.

As more sand sprinkled down on them, Miranda scooted away from the light. With all her other troubles, more sand in her eyes was the last thing she wanted.

Other than the beam of light coming from above, the place was eerily dark and cavernous around them.

As Miranda's gaze continued adjusting to the dim space, she glanced around. An old blanket lay on the floor. A broken headboard leaned against a wall. Mounds of sand drifted in the corners. The place smelled like the sea, like dankness, like . . . a buried prison.

On the other side of the space, a door came into view.

A door?

She scanned the space further. Actually, there were three doors total along the walls. And . . . a large window? What sense did that make?

Thaddeus let out a grunt—he must have noticed them at the same time she did.

"My nephew watches that show—*Stranger Things*," Thaddeus muttered. "And I feel like we've just fallen into the Upside Down."

Miranda shivered, halfway expecting a monster to jump from the shadows at any moment. "I couldn't agree more."

The only other questions on Miranda's mind were: Was Brian the person who'd knocked her out? Or had she stumbled upon a place someone hadn't wanted found?

CHAPTER THREE

THE BAD FEELING continued to grow in Thaddeus' gut.

First, he'd seen the man running.

Then he'd learned someone had hit Miranda and knocked her out.

Now this . . . this *pit*, for lack of a better word, had appeared out of nowhere.

This island . . . he'd thought it would be peaceful. But, so far, it held trouble—and not just because Miranda was here.

He reached for his phone, but it wasn't in his pocket. He must have dropped it when he fell. He glanced on the ground, kicking around some sand until he spotted it.

Once in hand, he glanced at the screen.

It was just as he thought—he had no service down here and no way of calling for help.

Miranda reached for her back pocket and frowned. "My phone is gone." She looked around for it. "I don't see it anywhere."

"Maybe it fell out earlier." He let out a sigh and glanced up. "As much as I'd love to figure out exactly where we are, we need to get out of here before that storm comes. I'm just not sure how."

"Can't we just climb out? I can stand on your shoulders, pull myself out, then help you."

Thaddeus stared at Miranda, seriously doubting the idea that she could pull him out. She probably weighed a hundred thirty pounds. He'd most likely end up pulling her back in instead.

But if Miranda got out . . . then at least she could run for help.

She might not like him, but certainly she wouldn't leave him here without telling someone what had happened . . . right?

"It's worth a shot, especially since we don't know how secure this structure is—or even *what* it is. Whatever way we can get out of here the most quickly, let's do it."

But he stared at the doors in the distance. If this plan failed, he'd try them next. He didn't think any of the doors led outside, not considering the massive dune above them. The dimensions didn't line up.

"I just want to get out of here."

As Miranda said the words, the light caught her face, and Thaddeus sucked in a breath.

Miranda Stewart was just as stunning as he remembered.

His gaze stopped on her lips, and he remembered the kiss they'd shared.

They'd connected in a way Thaddeus had never experienced before.

Then real life had happened . . . and he'd discovered that Miranda Stewart wasn't the woman he'd thought.

He frowned at the memories.

Instead of dwelling on that disappointment any longer, Thaddeus leaned down and braced himself to be used as a human ladder.

After only a moment of hesitation, Miranda scrambled onto his back almost as if climbing on for a piggyback ride. Then she placed a foot on his hip and tried to stand.

Instead, she began to tumble.

Quickly, Thaddeus grabbed her hands and helped her find her balance.

"Looks like you need more circus training." He

raised an eyebrow, trying not to be too amused in the dire situation. "Of course, that would require commitment."

Thaddeus frowned at his words. He shouldn't have said them.

But still . . . how could they have had such an incredible time together one moment and then a few weeks later, she was committed to someone else?

Everything Miranda had told him that night was clearly fabricated.

"Just be patient with me." Determination edged her voice. "And what are you talking about with that commitment comment?"

"Nothing." He winced at the question, still regretting the jab. He didn't usually let himself react emotionally. As an FBI agent, he had the fortitude and experience to remain distanced. He took a few deep breaths and tried to get himself in the right mind frame. "You can do it. Just take your time."

She attempted to climb again, her knees digging into his back.

As Thaddeus leaned down and glanced forward, his breath caught.

Soda cans littered the floor—soda cans that didn't look particularly old.

In fact, by their appearance it almost looked like someone had recently used this space.

But this building was buried. How was that possible?

The apprehension between Thaddeus' shoulders pulled tighter as the questions continued to pile in his head.

"How are you doing?" Thaddeus' strained voice couldn't be contained as Miranda's feet dug into his side.

"I'm . . . going to need . . ." It almost sounded like she gritted her teeth with the effort. "To stand on your shoulders."

He'd expected that. "Go ahead. I'll be here to catch you if you fall."

"Did you say, 'if you call'?"

"If I call? What?" Was the bump on this woman's head affecting her? Or had she just taken a jab at him? Sure, he hadn't called her after their date, but she'd given him a good reason not to.

"Never mind." As Miranda tried to put her foot onto his shoulder, she stumbled forward instead.

Thaddeus braced himself, ready to grab her before they added another emergency to an already tense—and dangerous—situation.

AIR SURROUNDED MIRANDA AGAIN.

She braced herself for the impact with the floor below.

She remembered the feeling well since she'd just experienced it only five minutes ago.

But before she landed, something caught her.

Thaddeus caught her—just as he'd promised.

She nestled in his arms, their faces dangerously close. She had instinctively circled her arms around his neck, and his solid chest promised an extra measure of protection.

As she glanced into his probing gaze, the air left her lungs.

He hadn't let her fall.

She shouldn't be surprised.

But after years of being let down by men, who could blame her for doubting? Besides, Thaddeus hadn't done what he'd promised when he'd left her in a "kiss and run" situation. They'd kissed that night and then . . .

She'd never heard from him again, despite his promise to keep in touch.

That wasn't how she operated. She was the type

of girl who liked commitment along with kisses, not cheap little flings that toyed with her heart.

But her love life—or lack thereof—wasn't her biggest problem right now.

Miranda cleared her throat, hoping the moment of attraction didn't show in her gaze. There was a difference between being attracted to someone and liking them.

And she *definitely* didn't like Thaddeus Blackwell.

"Thank you," she finally forced out.

Thaddeus set her on her feet. "You're welcome."

She glanced around the creepy space surrounding them and shivered, inadvertently scooting closer to Thaddeus again. "My plan isn't going to work, is it?"

He shook his head, a grim look on his face. "It was a good try. But I think we need to brainstorm more ideas here."

As Thaddeus said the words, the wind blew, sending more sand into the space.

Fear seemed to strangle Miranda.

What if sand continued to fill this space until they were buried alive?

The strangling fear turned into a clawing panic.

Her gaze swung around as her pulse quickened and her lungs tightened.

They had to get out of here.

Now.

Otherwise, this place just might end up being their grave.

CHAPTER FOUR

THADDEUS SAW panic flash through Miranda's gaze, and he knew he had to keep her calm or the situation would worsen.

"We'll find another way out of here," he assured her.

She ran a hand through her hair, her earlier confidence seeming to fade. "There are no other ways out of here."

"Someone's been coming and going." He nodded toward the cans on the ground.

She followed his gaze and gasped. "Those look . . . new."

"Exactly."

"But . . ." A knot twisted between her eyes.

"It's good news. It means someone has been

managing to get in and out of this place. So can we. We need to keep a cool head, though."

Miranda stared at him a moment, something uncertain fluttering through her gaze, before nodding. "Yes, right. Of course. A cool head."

Even as she said the words out loud, Thaddeus knew she hadn't fully embraced the concept yet. Fight or flight had kicked in—and she wanted to flee.

The problem was—fleeing was impossible.

"Maybe there's something in here that will help us get out," he finally said.

Miranda shivered and scooted closer to him, pulling her flannel shirt up higher around her burgundy-colored tank top. "Like what? Where are we even?"

"That's a great question." Thaddeus pulled out his phone again and, using his flashlight app, he shone the beam around the space.

At first, he'd thought maybe this could be an old bunker as Miranda suggested. But the doors in the room didn't fit how he envisioned a bunker. Nor did the insides of this place with its dingy plaster walls.

"That looks like a painting of the beach." Miranda pointed at something near her feet. "It reminds me of something you might see in a bedroom at an old beach house."

She was right. This space did appear to be an old bedroom.

More questions rose in his mind.

As he shone his light, he stopped at the second door. That had to be a bathroom.

And the third door . . . maybe it led outside. At least, maybe it had at one time.

Part of him wanted to explore this place. But the other part of him knew that they needed to get out before it turned dark. Before the storm came and the wind blew more sand inside or rain flooded the room.

Maybe if he opened one of those doors, he'd discover something that could help them escape.

Was it too much to hope for a ladder?

Probably.

Thaddeus reached for the door anyway.

Before he could open it, a noise sounded from the other side.

Was someone in the other room?

That's what it sounded like.

But Thaddeus needed to find out.

They didn't have any other options.

MIRANDA WATCHED as Thaddeus reached for the door handle again.

"What are you doing?" Miranda whispered, her words quick and low.

"I need to find out what that noise is."

She grasped his arm. "But what if someone is in there? Someone . . . *bad*? Or *something* bad?"

Part of her was envisioning monsters, even if she knew it was illogical.

"I'll be careful. I *am* an FBI agent. And I have my gun with me, just in case."

"Thaddeus . . ." Her voice sounded strained as she tugged at his arm.

He turned toward her, compassion rich in his gaze. "I promise that I won't make any sudden moves or do anything to put you in danger. Okay?"

Miranda tried to swallow, but her throat felt swollen. "You don't understand. If something happens to you, I'll be stuck down here alone. That's not okay."

Thaddeus stared at her, and Miranda realized how her words had probably sounded.

"Plus, I don't want anything to happen to you," she added. "Of course."

He offered a weary smile. "Grant is out looking for you also. When he doesn't hear from me, he'll come out this way. Okay? Someone will find us eventually."

She supposed his words made sense. Reluctantly, Miranda let go of his arm.

"Stay behind me," Thaddeus said and waited for her to scoot back a little.

She did. But she could hardly breathe as he shoved some sand aside and slowly opened the door.

She wasn't sure what she expected.

Bats to fly out.

The thug who'd hit her head to lunge toward them.

Mysteries from a secret world to be unleashed and change the fate of mankind as they knew it.

Okay, that last one had been overly dramatic. She'd been reading too many sci-fi novels lately. But still . . .

Instead, as the door swung open, silence stretched through the air.

The quiet was almost worse than any of the scenarios Miranda had envisioned.

What had caused the noise in the other room?

An animal? A person?

Was this living being hiding now, just waiting to jump out and take them by surprise?

Immediately following the silence was the scent of . . . decay. No, it was worse than decay.

What was that smell? Had some type of sea creature managed to get trapped inside and die? Or what if one of the wild horses on the island had fallen through the structure also?

Panic raced inside her at the thought of an animal suffering.

She prayed that wasn't the case.

As Thaddeus slipped inside, Miranda remained directly behind him—practically stuck to him with Super Glue, for that matter.

There was no way he was leaving her alone in this creepy space.

Miranda had been praying earlier that she could keep her dignity around the man.

Well, that hope was gone now.

Long gone.

"Do you see anything?" she whispered.

"Not yet."

As Thaddeus stepped deeper into the space, Miranda remained attached to his arm. His very muscular arm—not that the fact was important right now. But she did find reassurance in his strength.

She scanned the room, following the beam of Thaddeus' flashlight.

The space looked much like the one they'd fallen into. An old comforter rested halfway across an old mattress, a detached headboard leaned against the wall, a sand-covered dresser stood off to the side.

Were they in an old motel?

That's almost what this reminded Miranda of.

But . . . why would a motel be under a sand dune? What sense did that make?

Thaddeus' muscles tensed beneath her fingers.

He'd seen something, hadn't he?

Please, not an injured horse.

Or a gunman.

Or the entrance to the underworld.

"Thaddeus?" Her voice came out just above a squeak.

When he didn't say anything, Miranda peered around him.

That's when she saw two legs protruding from behind the dresser.

Her scream cut through the air as she realized exactly what she was looking at.

A dead body.

CHAPTER FIVE

"STAY THERE." Thaddeus stretched his hand behind him, motioning for Miranda to stay back.

He wasn't sure exactly what he was about to encounter—but he knew he didn't want Miranda to see it up close.

Ordinary people shouldn't see dead bodies.

No one should, for that matter. But at least he'd been trained. He knew what to expect.

Using his light, he crept closer and peered on the other side of the dresser.

He sucked in a breath.

A dead man.

With a gaping bullet wound in his chest.

Even worse, the man didn't appear to have been here for too long.

A day or two, based on what Thaddeus knew about decomposition.

He'd smelled the scent of decay as soon as he'd opened the door. But he'd never imagined this.

The bad feeling in his gut churned harder.

"Well?" Miranda's voice came out shaky.

Thaddeus purposefully used his body to block her line of sight.

He needed to get Miranda out of here before she panicked any more. But first, he snapped a few pictures to show Grant.

He strode across the room, took her arm, and turned her. "There's nothing you need to see."

Her face paled as her hand rushed over her mouth in horror. "You mean it's . . ."

He didn't speak until they were in the other room with the door closed. "It's a dead man."

There was no need to hide the truth from her. The situation they were in . . . it was dire.

"What were the sounds we heard?"

Thaddeus' gut churned harder. "That's an excellent question. Maybe there's an animal in another part of this building."

"Or someone else is down here."

He didn't respond. Clearly, someone had gotten

that body down here somehow. Was there another entrance?

He kept those thoughts quiet for now.

"I can't believe this." Miranda began pacing, her motions frantic. "What are we going to do?"

"The last thing we need to do is panic."

"How can I not panic? Did he just die? Was that the sound we heard?"

Thaddeus shook his head. "I don't know what that sound was. But it wasn't him. He's been dead for several hours, at least."

"How did he die? Could you tell?"

"He was shot."

She paused and buried her face in her hands. "None of this makes sense."

Part of Thaddeus wanted to step forward and comfort her in her distress. But he wasn't sure his touch would be welcome. The most logical thing would be to keep his distance. To remain friendly but professional.

She lifted her head, sucked in a deep breath, and then released it. Finally, she turned toward him. "Do you think this is an old motel?"

He glanced at the floor as the light from above glinted off something. He reached down and picked it up. It appeared to be a key with the numbers 128 and the words "The Sand Spur" on a black tag attached to it.

"I'd say a motel is a good guess."

"How in the world would a motel get buried beneath a sand dune?" Disbelief stretched through Miranda's voice—disbelief that echoed Thaddeus' own thoughts.

"That's something we'll have to figure out later. But I have a feeling that door we opened led into an adjoining room—and the others probably lead to a bathroom or a hallway."

To test his theory, he went and opened the second door.

An old bathroom—and a putrid scent—greeted him. He quickly shut that door and pulled on the third one. But this door wouldn't budge. The dented frame at the top had most likely crushed it in place.

"I can't believe this." Miranda rubbed the sides of her arms. "We have a wedding to prepare, and now we're stuck in an old motel buried beneath the sand dune. None of my friends will ever believe this story."

Thaddeus wanted to disagree with her, but none of his friends were going to believe this story either. However, in order for his friends to have the option of believing, it meant he needed to get out of here alive to tell them about it.

Using his boot, Thaddeus moved aside a few more things on the floor—some splintered wood that made it appear a table had once been where they stood, a towel, another broken picture frame.

Beneath them, he saw a metal box.

He shoved his phone back in his pocket. Carefully, he picked up the metal box, letting a few shards of glass and sand fall to the floor. He carried the box to the burst of light coming from above them and opened it.

As he did, Miranda reached down and picked up something also. She held it up. "A fountain pen. It looks kind of unique."

He glanced at the silver pen that shimmered with hints of purple and turquoise and shrugged. "I guess."

"I have this theory that a person can never have enough pens. Plus, this could come in handy in case I need to write my last will and testament while we're down here."

As she shoved it into her pocket, Thaddeus glanced at the metal box.

A bundle of papers had been stuffed inside.

"What is it?" Miranda leaned beside him to examine the contents.

"I have no idea. It looks like a map to something. A list of names. Maybe they're guests who stayed here."

"Maybe." Miranda leaned closer and frowned as she studied them. "But why would someone put a list of guests in a metal box in a motel room? Besides, wouldn't the ink be faded after all this time? I mean, I'm guessing this place has been under ground for several years now."

"Good point."

She glanced up, her gaze locking on his. "Could these be clues that are somehow connected with the dead man?"

Thaddeus stared at them a moment before shrugging. "It's a possibility."

As he leaned closer, the light above them shifted.

Was the storm on top of them now? Had clouds caused the shadow?

As Thaddeus looked up, a masked figure wearing all black looked down on them.

"Hey!" Thaddeus shouted.

The next instant, something covered the hole.

The light disappeared.

He and Miranda were trapped inside . . . and the

chances of Grant finding them now had greatly diminished.

MIRANDA SWALLOWED a scream and bolted back as talons of darkness fully gripped them.

"Hey!" Thaddeus shouted again, his hands cupped around his mouth. "What are you doing? You don't want to do this!"

His words did no good.

Miranda heard more movement—the movement of someone covering their escape route with sand.

Their only exit had vanished.

No one would ever find them now.

Her throat burned as she suppressed the cry wanting to escape.

She still gripped those papers they'd found in the metal box. Quickly, she folded them and shoved them into the back pocket of her jeans, somehow knowing she might be able to use them later.

If she survived.

The room grew quiet.

She could no longer see or hear Thaddeus.

She sucked in a breath.

"Thaddeus?" Her voice almost sounded childlike even to her own ears.

"I'm right here. Are you okay?"

"Yeah . . . I'm okay. Just scared."

A light popped on, and Thaddeus' shadowy figure appeared.

He reached out a hand for her. Without hesitation, Miranda stepped into his arms. Suddenly, their past didn't matter.

Only their survival did.

"We're going to figure this out," he murmured.

"Someone just trapped us down here to die." Her voice quivered. "And if the hole is covered up, how will Grant ever find us?"

He didn't say anything until finally he murmured, "We'll figure out something."

Miranda drew in a deep breath and released it, trying to keep calm. But panic relentlessly chased her until her head felt like it was spinning.

"Are we going to run out of air?" She prayed Thaddeus had a reassuring answer. An honest answer also. That they were one and the same.

"No, because we're going to get out of here."

"But—"

"No buts. We have to stay positive."

She drew in another deep breath and tried to

focus on replaying his declaration in her mind. *We're going to get out of here. Stay positive.*

Still holding her with one arm, Thaddeus shone his light around the room again, stopping on a dresser in the distance. "We can move that. I can use it like a ladder, see if I can shove the board covering the hole out of the way, and we can climb out."

Just as he said the words, thunder rolled above them.

Miranda jumped closer to Thaddeus, her heart pounding out of control.

At once, his leathery scent filled her.

She'd loved that scent. She'd craved it after she left Austin, where they'd had their one date together.

But Thaddeus had only been after a fling, and Miranda had been dumb enough to fall for his charm.

She'd been so heartbroken when she hadn't heard from him afterward that she'd run into the arms of Brian Bowers.

Brian proved to be an even bigger mistake than Thaddeus.

Miranda just couldn't win when it came to men.

But none of that would matter if she ended up dead.

As the thoughts raced through her head, sand

began pouring in from where the hole had once been. Were the edges of the hole collapsing? It was the only thing that made sense.

The pouring quickly became a cascade that turned into an avalanche.

Miranda gasped.

Their time was running out—she felt like she was trapped inside an hourglass.

ALARM RACED through Thaddeus as he realized there was more than enough sand on the dune to fill the room up—with them inside.

They didn't have much time. The storm outside would only speed up the process.

Reluctantly, he let go of Miranda and hurried toward the dresser. Using his hip, he gave the piece a good shove. The furniture felt solid and heavy.

Now he just needed to move it under the opening so he could boost himself up and out the hole.

In theory.

The pouring sand had slowed down. They needed to act before the situation got any worse.

He shone his light across the room at Miranda,

who stood right where he'd left her, her face abnormally pale—something he could see even in the dim light. Maybe if she was given a task, that would give her less time to think about her worst-case scenarios.

"Miranda, I need you to grab the other side of this."

Her entire body trembled, and, for a moment, Thaddeus feared she'd fall apart on him.

Instead, she sucked in a deep breath before scrambling to meet him on the other side of the dresser.

He needed to get her to focus. "I know you're frightened. But we don't have a lot of time here. So, we're going to need to move quickly. Understand?"

Her gaze flickered back to him, and she stared a moment before nodding. "I understand."

He placed his phone, light up, on top of the dresser, knowing that the total darkness would only increase her panic.

"Now, pick up that end of the dresser and let's move it," he instructed. "We need to place it under the opening we fell through so we can climb out. Okay?"

Miranda stared at him another moment and then nodded. "Okay."

She lifted the other end and slowly stepped back.

They finally got the dresser into place beneath the hole in the roof—the one now covered and piled on top with sand.

Thaddeus prayed their plan worked—because he'd never imagined having a coffin the size of a hotel room.

CHAPTER SIX

"THADDEUS . . ." Miranda stared at him, not bothering to hide the fear in her eyes.

He moved closer and gripped the sides of her arms as if trying to drive home his point before he totally lost her. "This is what we're going to do. I'm going to climb on top of this and see if I can push that board aside and get out."

At once, memories of Brian pummeled her thoughts. Memories of being abandoned. Of almost losing her life at the hand of a robber while her boyfriend fled without her.

"You're going to leave me down here?" Her voice cracked as she stared at him.

Even though the one person she should have

been able to trust back home in New York had completely failed her, she had to remember that didn't mean everyone would.

Still, she had no reason to think that Thaddeus wasn't like the rest of the men in her life.

Between Thaddeus' rejection, and Brian's and her father's abandonment, she'd lost all hope.

"When I get out, I'll lean down and pull you out, okay?" His gaze locked with hers.

Miranda stared at him a moment before nodding. Despite her fears, she didn't have much choice right now but to trust him. "Okay."

"I need you to hold my phone for me so I can see what I'm doing."

"Got it."

Thaddeus seemed to reluctantly let go of her arms. The next instant, he handed her his phone with the flashlight app on and then scaled the dresser. He carefully balanced himself on top and extended his arms above him.

Her heart pounded as she waited to see what would happen next.

She could trust Thaddeus. Right?

Her heart continued to race.

She watched as Thaddeus tried to find a grip on

the board. His muscles flexed and his teeth appeared gritted with concentration.

He grunted as he gave it a shove.

The board moved about an inch.

She held her breath as she continued watching.

He pushed the board again, and it continued to move slightly. Each time, sand cascaded inside, showering over him. The sand was followed by rainwater, which dripped into the space at a steady rhythm.

Once a large enough opening appeared, Thaddeus tested the edge to see how reliable it was.

Miranda held her breath, wondering if he'd be able to do this or not.

The next moment, his hands gripped the sides of the opening. He swung his legs up and caught his feet on the rim. Then he arched his back and shifted his legs through.

Miranda closed her eyes and prayed no more of the ceiling caved in and sent him toppling back into their prison.

When she glanced up again, Thaddeus was gone.

The hole was empty except for the rain pouring inside.

Her throat tightened.

What if her worst fears came true and Thaddeus left her here alone?

What if he disappeared from her life again, just like he had after Austin?

Emotions clogged her throat until she could hardly breathe.

Then that pounding question replayed in her mind, the one she'd been trying for so long to silence.

What if no one thinks you're worth enough to be loved?

"STEP ONE COMPLETE." Thaddeus lay on his stomach, leaned into the hole, and reached his hand down for Miranda.

As he did, rain pummeled his back, and the wind swept over him, bringing a smattering of sand into his face.

But at least he was out of that dungeon-like hole.

Now he just needed to ensure Miranda got out also.

She peered up at him, her eyes wide with unreadable emotions—maybe even glimmering with tears.

Tears? He thought she'd be relieved. But those almost looked like tears of sorrow.

He'd figure that out later . . . maybe.

Then again, when had he ever been able to figure out women?

He'd thought he'd understood Miranda, but he'd been totally wrong.

"I need you to stand on the dresser, Miranda," he called down to her. "I'm going to pull you up."

She glanced at the furniture and then at the hole. "Are you sure you're going to be able to do that?"

"I will. I'm not going to leave you."

Her shoulders seemed to soften at his words.

Had she really thought he would leave her here? What kind of man did she think he was, anyway?

The next moment, she shoved his cell phone into her back pocket before scrambling on top of the dresser. She found her balance with surprising ease before reaching up.

But her arms weren't long enough to touch the edge of the hole.

Thaddeus leveraged the upper half of his body as he reached toward her. "You're going to have to take my arm with both of your hands. Then I'll pull you out. It may not be pretty, but we're going to get this done."

"But . . ." Doubt glimmered in her gaze.

"You can do this, Miranda. I believe in you."

After a moment of quiet, she nodded. Then she reached forward.

Thaddeus caught her forearm in his. With her other hand, she grabbed the side of his arm and clung to him.

"I'm going to pull you up here. On the count of three. Okay?"

"Okay." But her voice sounded shaky, like she didn't believe it was possible.

"One. Two. Three." As Thaddeus said the last word, he tugged.

She rose from the dresser as rain pounded her face and thunder filled the sky.

Thaddeus gave another jerk, and she rose higher.

He was on his knees now. Both of her hands grasped his arm.

"One more pull," he yelled over the roar of the wind.

Thaddeus gave it everything he had as he propelled her upward.

She landed with a thud.

On top of Thaddeus.

But the relief that swept through him was so all-consuming he couldn't even move.

Until he realized his face was mere inches from Miranda's.

He grasped her arms, snapping himself out of his stupor. "Are you okay?"

Miranda nodded and rolled off him, lying faceup in the sand as she sucked in deep breaths of air.

She didn't seem to care about the rain that hit her skin. About the lightning that lit the sky. About the thunder that pounded overhead.

She only seemed to care that she was out of that old motel. Away from that dead body.

As grateful as Thaddeus was to be out of that space, they still had other problems.

For starters, they had to make sure the person who'd trapped them down there wasn't still lurking nearby.

Then they had to get to somewhere dry. It would be a long walk in this weather.

"Do you have my phone still?" he shouted over the wind.

She reached into her pocket and handed it to him. But when he looked at the screen, he saw he had no service out here. He'd have to walk farther before he could call Grant and let his friend know what was going on.

Instead of worrying, Thaddeus prayed. He prayed that the worst of this disaster was over and for protection as they navigated their way back.

CHAPTER SEVEN

AS THADDEUS TRUDGED through the sand with Miranda, he glanced around, looking for any signs of trouble.

He knew that, most likely, the person who'd trapped them in that buried motel was long gone, especially considering the weather. But there was a chance the perpetrator could be lingering nearby, watching to make sure they didn't escape, desperate to silence them.

This whole situation felt surreal.

Thaddeus was so grateful they were out of that motel. The ceiling could have caved in at any time and taken both of their lives. They could have run out of air. They had no food or water. There was even a chance that no one would ever find them.

The whole situation had been potentially deadly.

But their ordeal was far from over. Thaddeus would have to report what he'd found to law enforcement—which Grant just happened to be. They'd need to come out here and investigate.

Especially that dead body.

But first, he and Miranda had to get out of this weather. He had to know she was safe before he took any more action.

The sand dune with its thick grains was large and difficult to navigate. Adding weather, dehydration, and exhaustion to that, only made their walk back to the Jeep more complicated.

He continually scanned everything around him, although it was mostly Miranda he worried about.

Thaddeus glanced back at her. She seemed to lag at least three or four steps behind as they walked against the wind and rain.

He reached behind him and offered his hand to keep her moving at a steadier clip—for purely practical purposes.

Miranda stared at him a moment, distrust staining her gaze. Why would she distrust him? She was the one who'd been deceitful.

In fact, she was a totally different person than he'd thought.

The Miranda he'd seen in New York was nothing like the Miranda he'd met in Texas. Not to mention the fact that she was dating someone else only a couple of weeks after they'd met.

Finally, as lightning flooded the sky, Miranda reached forward and slipped her fingers into his.

Thaddeus knew he shouldn't feel anything for this woman. But he'd be lying if he denied feeling a whiz of electricity rush through him at her touch.

Just like he had when she'd landed on his chest.

He'd gotten a whiff of her flowery perfume, and the scent had transported him back in time.

But he couldn't allow himself to go there.

The woman made his head hurt. Thaddeus couldn't figure her out—and he didn't need to.

He'd only be here less than a week and then he'd head back to Texas again. Miranda would be on her way back to New York. Back to her boyfriend.

Eventually, the two of them would forget they'd ever met, and they'd never see each other again. The end.

"How much longer?" Miranda yelled over the wind.

"We're almost there."

Thaddeus tightened his grip on her hand and continued forward. The wind was so strong. They'd moved downhill because of the storm—the last thing he needed was to be on the highest point when lightning struck. But water had pooled near the base of the dune, and it was rising rapidly.

Just as the thought went through his head, more thunder rumbled in the sky, the powerful sound almost encompassing the air around them.

Miranda quickened her steps until she was beside him. Until she was close.

Her eyes were so wide they were almost childlike as she leaned closer and muttered, "I don't like this."

"I'll get you back. Then you can take a warm shower and get something to eat. You're going to be fine."

"What about the body?"

"I'll tell Grant, and he'll check it out."

He paused, pulling Miranda to a stop beside him. A large pool of water stretched in front of them. It almost appeared the ponds from the salt marshes had joined with overwash from the ocean.

Thaddeus had no idea how deep it was—or if there was an undercurrent.

"Do you think it's safe?" Miranda shouted over the storm.

"We have to try to cross it. You just need to hold onto me. Okay?"

She stared at him a moment before nodding. "Okay."

He gripped her hand tighter as he took his first step. He didn't know this terrain. Didn't know all the dangers of this area.

But he wouldn't forgive himself if he did something to hurt Miranda—to hurt anyone.

Still, they couldn't stay out here during this storm. It wasn't safe, especially not if the person who'd trapped them was anywhere close.

His boots sank into the wet sand before the water nearly reached his knees.

This wasn't looking good.

But they only had to make it about ten feet.

As he took another step, the cold water reached his waist.

Would he have to swim across this?

He gripped Miranda's hand harder.

"We can do this!" he yelled over the storm.

She only nodded and pushed a piece of hair that had been plastered to her face out of the way.

Thankfully, as they continued forward, the water didn't get any deeper.

But he wouldn't relax until they were back at Abigail's place. Out here, too much could go wrong. They were easy targets.

They reached the other side and walked several more paces in silence.

Finally, as the wind and the rain cleared for a moment, Thaddeus spotted a vehicle in the distance.

But it wasn't his.

This vehicle had its headlights on as it headed toward them.

Was it Grant?

Probably.

But Thaddeus knew there was also another possibility. The possibility that whoever had tried to trap them in that old motel was coming back to silence them.

AS MIRANDA STARED at the headlights, her hope turned to fear.

Especially when she felt Thaddeus bristle.

Was that help coming for them?

Or was it someone more sinister?

Thaddeus tucked her behind him as he turned toward the vehicle.

But as the driver put down his window, Grant's face appeared. "I was wondering what happened to you. Hop in the backseat."

Relief flushed through her, especially when she saw Abigail's face appear next to Grant's.

Her friends were here. Maybe she and Thaddeus were actually safe—for now.

She'd been trying not to be a whiny baby, but her head hurt. Her hip ached. And she was so exhausted and thirsty.

Fear could take a lot of energy out of a person.

Thaddeus helped her into the truck before climbing in behind her and slamming the door.

"Are you two okay?" Abigail frowned as she looked back at them. "You're both soaking wet."

"It's a long story." Thaddeus rubbed his jaw and sighed. "A *really* long story."

"It sounds like it." Grant glanced at them in the rearview mirror. "I'm glad we found you. When you didn't answer my calls, Thaddeus, I didn't know what to think."

"I didn't get the chance to let you know I'd found Miranda. Have you two been out looking for her this whole time?"

"After I asked him to pick me up, yes," Abigail said.

"It's high tide tonight, and the water is rising, expected to get deeper," Grant added. "I'm glad we found you when we did."

"We are too," Thaddeus said. "I need to show you something on the other side of the dune."

"Can it wait until the storm clears?"

"I'm not sure." Thaddeus frowned, his gaze appearing weary. "How about if we get the ladies back to the house and then I'll explain what happened? With this storm, you're going to have trouble getting to the crime scene."

"The crime scene?" Grant glanced back.

"I'll tell you everything—as soon as Miranda is safe."

Warmth filled her chest when she heard the concern in Thaddeus' voice. But if she was smart, she'd nip any warm feelings in the bud. The last thing she needed was to put any hope in the idea she could have a future with Thaddeus.

He'd already proven that wasn't possible.

Abigail sent her a worried glance before nodding. "Whatever you guys need. I'm just glad that you're okay."

But were they okay? Miranda wondered.

Or had they just unleashed something . . . kind of like in the movie *The Mummy* when the plagues were released on everyone around . . . and it had happened after the hero and heroine had made a discovery that changed everything.

CHAPTER EIGHT

AN HOUR LATER, Miranda sat on the couch beside Abigail at her friend's sprawling, oceanfront house. Abigail's father had gifted her with the eight-bedroom home, which was located on an area of the island known as the North Banks, where the more upscale homes were located.

As Miranda and Abigail talked, Grant and Thaddeus had returned to check out the crime scene—if they could get to it. She hoped they could, but she knew the chances were slim. Too much was working against them.

As Miranda took a sip of her hot tea, she tried to push away her worry. But the task felt impossible.

"Grant and Thaddeus know what they're doing." Abigail patted her hand. "They'll be fine."

Miranda pushed a wet strand of hair out of her face. She'd taken a shower, changed clothes, and taken a Tylenol. She felt a little more human. But not much.

"It was so crazy down there." As Miranda said the words, images of that buried space filled her mind. Even the musty scent rushed back to her, followed immediately by the smell of decay—the odor of the dead body. "I've never experienced anything like it."

"You really think it was an old motel?"

Miranda shrugged. "I can't say for sure. Have you ever heard anything about something like that?"

Abigail frowned. "No, I haven't lived here long enough to know all the history of this place. Maybe Grant can find out some answers for us. Levi Sutherland would normally help—he's the chief law enforcement official on the island. But he's out of town for a funeral, and Grant is in charge until he returns."

"On the week before his wedding?"

"Grant insisted. You know how he is. He always thinks of others before himself. He insisted it would be fine." Abigail patted her arm again. "I'm just glad you're okay . . . and that Thaddeus was with you."

Miranda frowned at the thought of the man. "Me too . . . I guess."

Abigail leaned back and took a sip of her own tea. "By the way, I never did ask what happened between the two of you. I assumed if you wanted to tell me that you would."

That night of their date flashed back in Miranda's mind, and she sighed. "It's . . . complicated."

"You both just seemed to be hitting it off at dinner—so much so that you decided to hang out more afterward."

"I've never felt a connection like I did with him," Miranda admitted as her thumb rubbed the side of the coffee cup. "When we left, he actually took me to his favorite park. We sat outside and talked for nearly five hours."

"Five hours? It sounds like you two really did hit it off. It also sounds kind of romantic."

"It was. We even kissed . . . and it felt magical."

"So, what happened?"

"He promised to call, and he never did." As Miranda said the words, she kept her voice matter-of-fact even though her heart felt anything but.

Abigail's eyes widened. "What? Really?"

Miranda nodded. "Really. I waited and waited. But there was nothing. He must have decided that a long-distance relationship wasn't for him. Or, that *I* wasn't for him."

"That's disappointing."

"I know. I had him pegged all wrong."

"I'm sorry to hear that. Grant always says Thaddeus is a standup guy. He's known him since high school."

Miranda shrugged. "Well, other than him getting us out of this mess today, I haven't seen the standup side of him. However, he's the least of my problems right now."

Right now, she had to figure out the Brian situation. Had to figure out why someone had knocked her out on that sand dune. And she had to figure out her future.

Her editor had given her an ultimatum before Miranda left to come here.

Find another feature story to work on, or don't bother coming back.

If Miranda didn't have her career, then what did she have?

Based on her experience . . . nothing.

"SWEET?" Thaddeus repeated. "That's *not* what I would call Miranda."

"If you don't mind me asking, what happened between the two of you?" Grant asked as they rode the truck up the sand dune, trying to figure out a safe way around the water.

Thaddeus wasn't sure that was going to happen. But he knew they had to at least try.

The storm still raged around them, lightning cracking the sky and thunder rumbling through the air.

Thaddeus let out a sigh as he thought about his friend's question. "The two of us had an amazing evening together. I don't believe in love at first sight, but that's what it felt like. Miranda and I . . . we just clicked. Anyway, we said goodbye and promised to stay in touch."

"But?"

Thaddeus felt his chest tighten as memories filled him, each one feeling like a punch. "That same night was when Hoffer died."

His friend frowned as he gripped the steering wheel. "Oh, man. I heard about that. I'm so sorry. I didn't know the man myself, but he sounded like a good guy."

"He was." Thaddeus' throat tightened as he

remembered his partner. "The next couple of weeks were a blur of grief and . . . guilt, I suppose."

"Guilt?"

"I feel like I should have been able to help. I still do." The words sounded raw as they left Thaddeus' lips. He hadn't meant to dive into something so personal. But maybe it would be good to get it off his chest.

Grant glanced at him. "That's . . . tough. But you can't blame yourself for what happened. Simpson was the one at fault."

He ignored his friend's statement, unable to dive into all the logistics of the situation right now. It was far more complicated than his friend even knew.

"I decided I had the perfect cure for my grief," Thaddeus said instead. "I had some time off work, so I decided to surprise Miranda in New York. I figured it might make up for the fact that I hadn't had a chance to call her with everything going on."

"How did that go?"

Memories pummeled Thaddeus as he stared at the drizzles of rain running down the window. "I went to her office building with some flowers that cost entirely too much money. But Miranda was worth it, right? But, before I could even ask the receptionist where to find her, I spotted her outside. With another man."

"What?" Grant's voice rose in surprise.

Thaddeus nodded, wishing he could squelch the bad memory. "She looked happy. She and this guy were holding hands and laughing. The man was pretty much my complete opposite—a city slicker businessman who appeared to be climbing the social ladder."

Grant frowned. "That doesn't seem like her—not that I know her that well. But Abigail always talks about how sweet and personable Miranda is. She says she's super down-to-earth."

Thaddeus narrowed his eyes as he remembered the moment. "It was almost like Miranda had transformed into a different person. Gone was the girl who said she liked to wear jeans and comfortable shirts. The girl who liked to talk about her favorite sci-fi movies and books. Who laughed so hard she snorted. This Miranda was dressed in designer clothes from head to toe. She was sophisticated—"

"Wait—you can identify designer clothes?"

Thaddeus shrugged. "Not always. But this time I could. Anyway, Miranda just looked so sophisticated and like a city girl who belonged in New York. Who belonged with someone equally as sophisticated and city-oriented. If I hadn't known it was her, I might have thought she had a twin."

"She doesn't." Grant shook his head. "Man, I'm sorry. Did you ever talk to her?"

"I figured there was no reason to. She'd already moved on and was seeing someone else. What was there to talk about?"

"Are you sure that guy wasn't just a friend?"

Thaddeus frowned. "He kissed her on the cheek —but not like a friend would."

"Abigail told me Miranda dated someone for a few months but that they'd broken up. I don't know any other details."

Why did that thought intrigue Thaddeus? It shouldn't.

He pushed it aside. "Anyway, I went back to Texas and moved on."

"By dating someone else?"

"No, I haven't met anyone else who's caught my attention."

Grant nodded as they bounced over the sand, his windshield wipers swinging back and forth in front of them. "Well, I hope things go well with you two this week."

"I'm sure they'll be fine." The last thing Thaddeus wanted was for the tension between him and

Miranda to ruin his friend's wedding. Thaddeus wouldn't let that happen.

Suddenly, Grant stomped on the brakes and frowned.

Thaddeus followed his gaze and saw what almost looked like a river in front of them.

"It doesn't look like we're going to be getting back to that dead body tonight," Grant said. "This is the best spot to cross, and it's filled with water. It looks at least three feet deep."

"So, what do we do?"

"Right now, I say we stop and pick up the Jeep. We don't want floodwaters to ruin it. Then we'll come back first thing in the morning. I can't put my guys at risk. It doesn't sound like the elements are going to work in our favor as far as getting down into that hole this evening anyway. It's too risky because of the darkness, the storm, and the unstable nature of the dune itself."

Thaddeus nodded, knowing his friend was right. He'd already shown Grant the pictures he'd taken.

But Thaddeus was anxious to see that body again . . . and to figure out what was going on.

Finding answers was a much safer bet than thinking about Miranda.

CHAPTER NINE

AN HOUR LATER, everyone was back at Abigail's house. One of Abigail's friends, Emmy Sutherland, had stopped by with some chicken pot pie, sweet tea, and chocolate chip cookies.

From what Thaddeus understood, Grant had asked Emmy to come by and share whatever she knew about Knobs Hill with them. The food had been an unexpected treat.

They all sat around the table now, enjoying their food and drinks as Abigail filled Emmy in on what had happened. The scent of the butter-crusted pie mingled with the savory aroma of gravy and chicken. The warm meal was a nice reprieve as the storm continued to rage outside.

"It must be the old Sand Spur Motel," Emmy said.

"How in the world did the motel end up under a sand dune?" Grant took a sip of his tea as he waited for an answer. "I didn't even think there were motels on this island."

"It was the only one, and locals hated it." Emmy sliced her fork through the air as she emphasized her words. "It was only allowed to be built because Arnold Hillsdale, the county superintendent at the time, had a personal stake in the place. Most people were happy to see it go."

"How long ago was this?" Thaddeus asked.

"That place has been closed down for . . . oh, I don't know . . . probably ten years," Emmy said. "The motel was a real eyesore located right at the base of the sand dune. However, every year, the dune shifts a little bit to the west. It's all based on the current and the wind direction and storms. This whole island shifts, for that matter. It's really nothing more than a big sandbar."

"That's not comforting." Miranda stabbed a piece of gravy-covered chicken and frowned.

Grant glanced at her and shrugged. "I thought that also when I first moved here. But Cape Corral has been here for hundreds of years, so I wouldn't worry about it too much."

"Go on," Thaddeus prodded, anxious to hear more. He took another bite of his food as he waited. He hadn't realized he was so hungry.

"Sand began piling up all around the motel," Emmy continued. "In fact, the last few years the place was open, every room came with a shovel so guests could get rid of any sand that encroached on their rooms."

"Now *that's* a story." Thaddeus tried to imagine being a guest back when the place was open.

"Everyone thought there would be more time to demolish the place. But around ten years ago, a huge hurricane swept over the island. Everyone had to evacuate because we weren't sure what was going to be left of this place after the category four storm."

"Is that the storm that washed out the bridge leading to the island?" Miranda's rapt attention seemed to be on the conversation as curiosity filled her gaze.

"Actually, that was a different one—it's only been a couple of years since that happened," Grant said. "Storms can reshape this whole area."

"Anyway, we didn't know what to expect when we got back to the island," Emmy said. "We did lose some homes close to the shore. Several people lost their roofs or their HVAC units. But when we came back to that area of Knobs Hill—"

"Is that the name of the sand dune?" Thaddeus asked.

"Oh, yeah. I thought you knew that. It used to be the largest on the East Coast until Jockey's Ridge in Nags Head took over the title. Anyway, we realized that the wind was so strong it had shifted the sand dune at an accelerated pace. The entire motel was now covered."

Miranda leaned closer, appearing absolutely fascinated by the story. "Why didn't anyone uncover it?"

"It wasn't that easy." Emmy took a long sip of her iced tea before continuing. "I know it sounds like it might be. But sand is heavy and hard to manage. My father was the chief law enforcement officer back then, and Levi had just started on the force. They tried for a while to dig out the place, but the motel must have been buried too deeply in the sand. They figured it really wasn't worth it in the long run and just let nature run its course. Besides, Knobs Hill became protected under the national park system not long after that, and now there are a lot more hoops to jump through."

"That's absolutely crazy." Thaddeus shook his head in disbelief.

"I know it sounds crazy, but it's true." Emmy's gaze shifted back and forth between all of them. "But now it sounds like they probably should have put in the time back then to uncover it. Sounds like someone is using it now to stage their crimes."

"That's definitely what it feels like," Thaddeus said.

The question was who? And was this person still on the island?

MIRANDA LISTENED with interest to everything Emmy had shared. The woman was a wealth of information—and a nice distraction from thoughts about Thaddeus.

She wished she had a pen and paper to take notes. As soon as she got back to her room, she would write down all the details she'd learned. As a reporter, she could smell a story a mile away—and this was definitely a story.

Maybe it was the one that would save her career even.

Miranda took another sip of her tea before

leaning forward, her thoughts still racing through the previous conversation. But it was more than the history of the place that had her fascinated.

It was the fact that Grant and Thaddeus hadn't been able to get back to the motel tonight to secure the crime scene.

"What if the person who left that body there comes to get it before you can make it back?" Miranda asked.

Grant glanced at the window just as lightning lit the outside. "I doubt someone's going to go out in these conditions."

Miranda rubbed the edge of her plate with her thumb as her thoughts raced. "There is one other possibility . . ."

Grant stared at her. "What's that?"

"What if there's a passageway that allows people to come and go from the motel whenever they want?"

His eyes narrowed with thought. "Why would you think that?"

"The body hadn't been there very long," Thaddeus said. "Someone either put him there or killed him there. We thought we heard someone else inside the space while we were trapped. There was another door, one we couldn't get open. I assumed it led to a hallway. Did the motel have outside room entrances?"

Emmy frowned and shrugged. "From what I remember, the entrances were on the interior, but I can't be a 100 percent sure."

Thaddeus' jaw visibly tightened. "We broke through the roof when we fell. It wasn't a normal entrance. There was no ladder to climb down, nothing to break our fall. There has to be another way in."

"I agree." Miranda nodded. "I remember hearing something breaking right before we fell in. I don't think that hole was there before that."

"Besides . . . I think we heard someone down there with us. When we went into the adjoining room, no one was there. Maybe they ran. I'm not sure. But we clearly heard something."

"I thought you said it was an animal?" Miranda stared at him, uncertain if she'd heard him correctly.

"I didn't want to freak you out."

Grant let out a breath and ran a hand over his face. "First thing in the morning, I'll see what I can find out. But I can't imagine where another entrance might be."

"Is there a survey of the property on file you can look at?" Thaddeus asked.

"There should be. I'll look for it. I'll also look through any missing persons reports from the area to see if we can ID the body." Grant glanced at Abigail. "This certainly isn't how I envisioned spending the week before our wedding."

"I'll be fine while you check things out." Abigail waved a hand in the air as if it wasn't a big deal. "I have Miranda here to keep me company. You just don't get yourself hurt. Understand?"

Grant gave her a salute, followed by a wink. "Understood."

This whole area captivated Miranda. It almost felt like she'd come to the Old West, even though she was still here on the Atlantic. But this island was just so isolated.

Not to mention full of cowboys, horses, and a justice system that seemed to almost be isolated to itself.

Then there was a motel buried under the sand.

As the others began to talk amongst themselves, Miranda leaned back and listened.

For a moment, she imagined what it would be like to live here.

Part of her was intrigued with the idea of small-town living. She liked the idea of people knowing her name. Of belonging. Of a simpler life.

It was the opposite of what she had in New York.

She longed to find a place where she fit. After her mom died four years ago, she'd felt so alone. That's when she'd really poured herself into her work. When she'd become even more determined to have a better run at life than her mother had.

But could she ever actually see herself living in a place like this? Although this story was unique, she couldn't imagine this island having enough stories to sustain a reporter full time.

Besides, as an entertainment reporter, Miranda was always on the go. Her job required her to do in-depth interviews. She often flew across the country so she could see her interview subjects on their home turf. Clearly, New York was the best place to be based, just for the ease of flying.

Even if she were to work remotely, the internet wasn't that great here on the island.

So why did a smidgen of disappointment hit her at the thought that making a change like that could never happen?

Emmy turned toward her, her eyes lighting with excitement. "By the way, Miranda. You're never going to believe this."

Miranda slowed her motions, her fork-laden hand suspended in midair. "Believe what?"

"Somebody stopped by the inn today, and he was asking about you."

Miranda felt the blood drain from her face. She set down her fork. "He was asking about me?"

"That's right. It was a man. It was dark outside, so it was hard to see him. But he said he came to town to talk to you. Are you expecting someone?"

She opened her mouth to speak, but no words came out.

Because all she could think about was that Brian had followed her.

CHAPTER TEN

THADDEUS WATCHED as Miranda's expression changed.

She was spooked.

But why?

Clearly, she wasn't expecting anyone to come looking for her here in Cape Corral. Thaddeus had been a federal agent long enough to know when someone was covering something up. But now wasn't the time to ask questions.

He sensed her discomfort and turned back to the rest of the group, ready to change the subject despite his curiosity.

"I'm willing to do whatever I can to help out with the investigation," he offered. "I know you have your own law enforcement here on the island, but I'm available if needed."

"I may just have to take you up on that." Grant pushed his empty plate away. "I definitely want you to lead me back to the area where you found the body."

"I'll do whatever you need." As Thaddeus said the words, he tried to remember any markers that might help him recall the exact location where they'd fallen into the motel. But all he remembered was the endless stretch of sand as he and Miranda had started toward safety and the long walk while battling the elements.

But he'd worry about that in the morning.

"I'm so glad you guys are okay." Abigail stood and began collecting the plates from the table. "How about if we get some dessert and then unwind? That dead body will be there in the morning, so there's no need to lose sleep over it now."

"That's right," Thaddeus said. "You two have other things to think about—starting with your wedding."

But even as he tried to sound lighthearted, his mind felt a million miles away.

Who could be asking around the island about

Miranda? Based on her reaction there had to be something up with that.

But mostly, his thoughts continued to drift back to that body they'd found.

Just what had happened here in Cape Corral?

And how much danger were he and Miranda still in?

AS MIRANDA LAY in bed that night, her thoughts continued to race.

It had to have been Brian who'd shown up at the inn. But why would he follow her all the way here?

Unless he wanted to teach her a lesson.

It *had* to be Brian. No one else made sense.

As the windows rattled with the wind and branches scraped across the glass, she pulled her blankets higher.

She was grateful to be staying here with an FBI agent as well as a local law enforcement official. The weather was so bad outside that Grant and Thaddeus had decided to sleep in the spare bedrooms here at Abigail's. Having the two of them here gave her a better sense of security.

But if Brian tried to make good with his threats . . . *I'll do whatever it takes to get you back.*

That might include hurting anyone who stood in his way.

She pressed her head farther into her pillow.

Still, how would he have found her here? She would have noticed him following her.

Besides, he wouldn't have trapped her in that old motel. There was no way he could have known she'd fallen through a collapsed roof into a buried building.

Had Miranda somehow gotten herself in the middle of two different sources of danger?

She turned over in bed again and pulled the covers up to her chin, trying to clear her thoughts. But it almost felt impossible.

Every time she closed her eyes, all she could see was that dead body. The fear she'd felt while trapped inside that space under the sand slammed back into her mind.

If Thaddeus hadn't found her when he did and Miranda had fallen into that old motel alone, there was a good chance she would have been trapped in that space . . . forever. It would have been her final resting place.

For that reason, she was thankful for Thaddeus.

His face raced into her mind. She'd seen the surprise in his gaze when Emmy mentioned someone stopping by asking about her. Thaddeus was almost too observant for his own good. But at least he'd quickly changed the subject.

The last thing Miranda wanted was for him to find out about Brian. Thaddeus had already rejected her once. There was no need for him to know what a string of bad relationships she'd had over the years, especially this latest one. It would only add to the humiliation she already felt when she'd realized how much more invested she'd been in pursuing something with Thaddeus than he'd been in return.

The sting was still there even after all these months.

She punched her pillow, hating the self-esteem war that raged inside her. On one hand, she'd graduated at the top of her class. She'd succeeded in almost anything she tried.

On the other hand, she'd allowed the actions of others to damage her sense of self-worth. She'd made poor relationship choices as a result. She'd gotten involved with people who put her down, among other things. Over the years, that had chipped away at her already vulnerable self-esteem.

She'd been a gangly child, quiet in large groups

but talkative around those who knew her. It was only once she was in college that she'd blossomed, so to speak. Even then, her focus had been on academics, which served her well in her career but also prevented her from dealing with the deeper issues she continued to battle.

But, right now, none of that mattered. When this wedding was over, Miranda would return home to her life in New York. She'd go back to her job. Her daily routine. But the thought wasn't as appealing as it probably should be.

How much longer could she live the stressful life she had in The Big Apple? The lifestyle she had to adopt in order to be successful was taking a toll on her. Something she once thought she'd find fulfilling hadn't turned out at all like she'd expected. Now it all just drained her and left her feeling empty.

She needed to make a change. But what could that change look like? A move to a new city? A new job?

She stared out the window again and let out a sigh.

As she did, an idea crept into her head.

What if she dug deeper and broke the story on this motel that had been buried beneath the sand? About the body found inside?

If she did, maybe she could move away from being an entertainment reporter and work on more hard-hitting investigative journalism instead. Her editor often accused her of being an investigative reporter at heart since Miranda had trouble only sticking to surface-level features. She always wanted to go deeper into people's lives.

Maybe this was her chance to prove herself as a journalist. To exit her current job.

Her editor required too much of her—and what Miranda offered was never enough. Plus, keeping up appearances could be so exhausting. How much longer could she continue holding onto her professional persona while hiding who she really was?

She knew she needed to give it a shot, that she'd fallen—literally—into this opportunity. She couldn't just pass it up.

She had to change something now or risk losing the real Miranda forever.

CHAPTER ELEVEN

"I COULDN'T SLEEP last night so I looked at missing persons reports from over the past couple of months," Grant started. "But I didn't find anything."

Thaddeus frowned, even though the news didn't surprise him. "I figured that would be a longshot. Nothing's ever that easy, is it?"

Before the sun had breached the horizon, Thaddeus and Grant had set out in Grant's truck to go to Knobs Hill. They'd brought a ladder and other gear they might need in order to go into the Sand Spur and retrieve that body. Another officer—Dash Fulton—was handling a domestic dispute at the moment, but he would be available later to lend a hand if needed.

Grant narrowed his gaze. "If someone on this

island murdered someone and left the body in the old motel, then you really have just opened up a can of worms, as the saying goes."

"No doubt about that. I didn't say this in front of the ladies because I didn't want to upset anyone—namely Miranda." Thaddeus frowned as he said her name. "But when I saw the body, I'm pretty certain this man had a snake tattoo that went around his arm and up his neck."

"I'll see if the tattoo matches anything on record."

The good news was that the storm had passed, the temperature was a balmy sixty-five, and sunshine was forecast for the rest of the day.

Thaddeus stared out the windshield as they bounced down the sandy road. In the distance, on the shoreline, a harem of wild horses roamed together. They sure were a beautiful sight. He thought Texas was beautiful—and it was—but this area was definitely something unique.

"That's not something you see every day." Thaddeus pointed to the horses.

"Actually, it is if you live here." Grant glanced at Thaddeus. "You know, we're looking to hire another law enforcement officer for the forestry division."

"Out here?" Thaddeus chuckled and looked back

at the horses again. "I don't know if things are quite exciting enough out on Cape Corral for me."

"Oh, you might be surprised at how exciting it gets," Grant murmured before shaking his head. "You might be *really* surprised."

Thaddeus didn't know about that. He couldn't imagine the sleepy little island having that much excitement. Yet another part of him imagined what it *would* be like to live here.

The slower pace. Being able to watch the waves in the morning. To breathe the fresh air.

Those things did have some appeal.

Plus, part of him wanted a fresh start after everything with Hoffer.

His heart thumped harder at the thought of his former partner and the betrayal that had followed everything that happened. His life seemed marred by betrayal lately, and it was enough to leave him uneasy. Miranda somehow seemed to bring it all to the forefront.

Part of him wanted to avoid her at all costs. But another part of him remained fascinated by the woman. And yet another part of him wanted to figure her out, to discover who she really was deep down.

His divided emotions swirled inside like a whirlpool.

She might be his toughest investigation yet—and the one he had no business getting involved in.

They reached Knobs Hill, and the truck's tires dug into the sand, practically crawling through it. Since this was an official law enforcement vehicle, they were permitted to drive on the dune.

Thaddeus knew the motel was at least a half a mile in. But out here, everything looked the same, unfortunately.

He glanced around. Even though last night's storm had subsided, pools of water had developed along the edges of the sand dune and in the crevices.

It almost looked like a small oasis in the middle of the desert.

"We have to be getting close," Grant muttered as he gripped the wheel.

"I agree." Thaddeus continued to scan the barren sandy landscape around them. "Just be careful. I'd hate for you to ride up on top of it."

"Me too. Let's park here and walk the rest of the way. Once we find the spot, we can move the truck closer." Grant stopped the truck on the hillside and shifted into Park. "Who would have ever thought when the hotel was still in operation that it would disappear like this one day?"

"How long ago was the Sand Spur built?" Thaddeus asked as they got out and began walking.

"I'd say thirty years based on what Emmy told us and the records I looked up last night." Grant shrugged. "It had thirty-two rooms. Two stories. Definitely nothing fancy."

They walked along the general vicinity of the hole, over indistinguishable drifts of sand.

But the spot was gone.

Thaddeus didn't see it anywhere, even though he knew they had to be within the right radius. The sand must have covered up the opening again. Or the person had come back to conceal the hole a second time. There was really no way to tell for certain.

Grant crossed his arms and shook his head. "This doesn't look good."

"This isn't okay." Thaddeus stared at the mass of sand in front of him, regret battering him. "I thought it was on this ridge. How is it possible that I can't find the spot?"

Grant placed a hand on his shoulder. "That's the nature of this place. Everything's always moving and shifting. It's not your fault."

"I should have paid more attention last night when we got out. I just had no idea that it would be gone like this." The thought of it flabbergasted him. If Thaddeus had known then what he knew now, he would have placed a marker at the spot. He would have done *something*.

"You had other things to think about. Things like survival."

Thaddeus bit down, his jaw hard with tension. "How do we find it now?"

Grant stared at the sand dune in front of him and let out a sigh. "That's a good question, and it's going to require some thought. We can't exactly start bulldozing this whole place. Not only would it be like searching for a needle in a haystack, but it could also be dangerous. Heavy equipment on top of this could be disastrous, and it could ruin any evidence that would be down there."

"I'm assuming that things like ground-penetrating radar aren't a possibility?" Thaddeus asked. "Or some type of land survey?"

"Ground-penetrating radar is a possibility, but it's a matter of when we could get someone out here who's skilled at using it. As far as a land survey . . . it would help us pinpoint the location of the motel, but there are permits we'd have to obtain and hoops we'd have to jump through in order to dig in this area. Knobs Hill is protected due to the wild horses. Besides, Mother Nature can be awful tricky when she wants to be. Something like this could take days if not weeks to find. Let's walk around a little more just to make sure we didn't miss anything."

As they reached the top of the dune, a noise cut through the air.

A gunshot.

Someone was shooting at them.

AFTER BREAKFAST, Miranda, Emmy, and Abigail gathered to put together some goody bags that would be given to everyone at the rehearsal dinner. The remaining scents of fresh-pressed orange juice along with homemade cinnamon rolls lingered in the air, and the open windows made everything feel more alive.

Miranda would never admit it to her friend, but, more than anything, she wanted to be out there investigating with Thaddeus and Grant. She wanted to see what else might turn up at the scene. Wanted to know if there was anything new.

She was even willing to spend time with Thaddeus if it meant finding answers—and that said a lot since the man was nowhere near the top of her list of favorite people to be around.

Another part of her couldn't bear the thought of ever going into that space again. Being trapped in the buried building had been something from her nightmares.

Still, her curiosity raced. She wanted answers.

She wanted to write a story on whatever was going on there.

Abigail was her first priority, however.

She turned her attention back to the present.

Abigail had turned on some country music as they worked.

"So, everybody in town is talking about what happened to you yesterday," Emmy said as she stuffed a bag with some Tylenol, hand sanitizer, personalized chocolate kisses, and tissues.

"Word travels fast, huh?" Small towns were totally different from what Miranda had grown up with. She'd always lived in a larger urban area.

As much as she wanted to solely focus on Abigail, she knew Emmy was a great resource as far as information about the island. Maybe she could honor Abigail *and* find out some answers right now.

"When we do get excitement around here, it's all

anyone talks about," Abigail explained. "It's been pretty quiet for the past several months. But hearing about the old Sand Spur Motel has piqued a lot of interest."

"I'm not sure that's a good thing." Miranda tried to push away the bad feelings simmering in her gut as she sat on the floor and passed her bag to Emmy in assembly-line fashion.

"Why?" Emmy asked. "Because of the dead body?"

Miranda nodded. "Exactly."

"Yeah, that's really creepy." Emmy raised her eyebrows. "I've lived on this island my whole life, and I just can't imagine who it might be. Then again, that area is pretty remote. I suppose anyone could have gone there and gotten themselves into trouble."

"So, neither of you have any guesses as to what might have happened?" Miranda was fishing for information for her possible article, but she was also genuinely curious.

"Maybe he was a pirate," Abigail suggested, adding a playful "argh" at the end.

"A modern-day pirate?" Emmy sounded skeptical. "They'd more likely die at sea."

"Maybe it's someone who wandered into Wash

Woods and got lost," Abigail suggested. "The spirit of the woods could have possessed them."

Miranda had no idea what Wash Woods was or what the legend behind the area might be. She'd save that question for later. She'd had her share of creepy locations since she'd arrived.

"Lost or not, someone shot the man," Miranda noted.

"Maybe he was a horse thief," Emmy suggested. "We've had a few of those around here. That's a good way to make enemies fast."

Miranda turned those ideas over in her mind. Maybe one of them was valid, but she had a feeling that wasn't the case.

After they stuffed the last bag, Miranda rose and stretched. As Abigail and Emmy continued talking, she wandered toward the sliding glass door and opened it, letting the fresh breeze flow over her. She stepped onto the balcony to catch a glimpse of the ocean.

Seeing it always made her feel better.

But instead of looking at the water, her gaze caught something else in the distance.

A figure stood near a black truck parked on the sandy road a couple of houses down.

A man.

Looking directly at her.

As soon as their gazes met, he jumped back into his truck and took off.

Miranda's heart pounded in her chest.

Was she imagining things or was that . . . Brian?

CHAPTER TWELVE

"WHERE ARE THE GUNSHOTS COMING FROM?" Thaddeus yelled as he scrambled behind the rise of the dune, Grant beside him.

"From the woods, I think."

Thaddeus' mind raced.

The only person who'd be shooting at them now was most likely the same person who'd trapped him and Miranda in the old motel last night.

He and Grant must be getting close to the spot they were looking for, and someone was desperate for them not to find that motel again.

He remembered the red tape Grant said they'd have to cut through in order to take extensive actions to find the old building. Just how long would that hold them up?

Another bullet sliced the air.

He and Grant exchanged a look. Without saying anything, they both knew what they needed to do.

At Grant's signal, they darted toward his truck and dove inside.

As they did, a bullet cracked one of the windows.

This guy wasn't giving up, was he?

Grant cranked the engine and charged toward the woods.

If they wanted answers, they had to catch this guy.

Thaddeus braced himself, waiting for more bullets to split the air.

But none came.

The guy was running, he realized. Their shooter didn't want to risk being caught.

Grant reached the edge of the woods and threw the truck into Park. He and Thaddeus jumped out, guns drawn, ready to find the shooter.

Tension threaded up Thaddeus' spine as he searched the thick woods edging the dune.

His instincts told him this guy escaped. But he needed to remain on guard. Assumptions could get him killed.

And him being killed would be no way to celebrate his friend's upcoming nuptials.

Several minutes later, he met Grant back at the truck. They both shared the same grim expression.

"He's gone." Grant rubbed his jaw as he shook his head. "He must have taken off the moment he saw us coming."

"But where did he go?" Thaddeus glanced at the sand dune behind him then at the woods in front. Granted, the trees and underbrush were thick in those woods. There were plenty of places to hide. But he didn't know the layout of this island well enough to form a complete picture.

"There are some houses on the south side of the dune," Grant said. "If this guy went deeper into the forest, he'd be in the heart of Wash Woods by now. Not a place you want to be without knowing what dangers to look out for."

"Wash Woods? What makes it dangerous?"

Grant shrugged. "The place has several legends surrounding it, legends that date back more than a century. There have also been some instances of quicksand in the area, and wild boars and snakes are plentiful. It's not really the kind of place people should want to hang out, but you'd be surprised at how many people we catch back there."

"Quicksand in North Carolina?"

"Believe it or not, it's true. Another officer, Dash, had some firsthand experience with it."

Thaddeus shook his head at the thought. "This place reminds me more and more of the island from that TV show *Lost*. You just never know what to expect. If a smoke monster appears, I'm out of here."

"You're telling me." Grant shook his head, almost looking weary. "Let me go talk to county officials and see if I can get a permit to start digging in this sand. Hopefully, they won't drag their feet too long."

"Let's hope."

"In the meantime, I'll get you back to the house. Thanks for your help today."

"Of course." But Thaddeus' stomach clenched. Going back to the house meant going back to see Miranda.

Was he ready for this?

———

MIRANDA TRIED to get the image of that man out of her head as she stood gripping the railing on the balcony.

Had it been Brian?

She couldn't say with 100 percent certainty. The man had been wearing a hat and sunglasses. But he'd been facing her, almost as if he'd wanted to make a statement.

Miranda shivered and prayed he hadn't followed her to Cape Corral.

"Everything okay out here?"

Miranda glanced back as Abigail stepped onto the balcony. Her friend had always formed an elegant figure with her slender build, her long brown hair flecked with gold, and her gentle smile.

Grant Matthews was a lucky man to have someone like Abigail in his life.

So was Miranda. Abigail had been a great friend throughout the years.

Miranda and Abigail had been friends since college. Back then, Miranda had been a different person. Except she wasn't. On the inside, she was still the same.

Maybe her outsides had been transformed, and she was no longer the plain Jane she'd once been. But she was still fighting a battle with self-esteem. Abigail had been her friend back when Miranda had practically been invisible, and she'd been her friend when Miranda had transformed into a shining star in her new life phase.

It didn't matter to Abigail how Miranda looked

or how successful she was. True friends like that were hard to find.

"I was just looking at the ocean. It's beautiful." Miranda didn't want to ruin her friend's upcoming wedding by discussing her problems.

"Yes, it is."

Miranda glanced behind Abigail. "Where's Emmy?"

"She had to take a phone call. She runs the inn in town and has to field questions from guests."

Kind of like the one from the man who'd shown up last night asking for Miranda.

She swallowed hard at the thought.

Just then, a white truck pulled up to the house.

Miranda's lungs froze at the sight of the unfamiliar vehicle. Was it . . . the shooter? Would he be brazen enough to simply pull up to the house?

As a man with shaggy blond hair stepped out, she released her breath.

"You look like you've seen a ghost. That's just Stephen, the pool and hot tub guy." Abigail let out a chuckle before wagging her eyebrows. "I do believe he's single, just in case you're looking or if you need someone to distract you from Thaddeus. Are beach bums your type?"

"No, thank you." Miranda shook her head. "I've had enough with relationships. I'm done."

How many times did men have to disappoint her before she realized that all the drama simply wasn't worth it? She didn't mind being single. In fact, she was content to be alone. For now, at least.

There was still part of her that wanted something like what Grant and Abigail had. She wanted a lifelong partner. Someone who understood her and supported her.

One day, she wanted kids and family vacations and piles of laundry to wash after a busy week of soccer and dance.

She wanted the life she'd never had growing up with a single mom and an absent father.

But she wouldn't sacrifice her peace of mind to obtain that.

"Brian was really that bad, huh?" Abigail asked quietly.

His image filled Miranda's mind, and she frowned. "He was definitely that bad."

"Well, there's always Thaddeus . . ." Abigail held onto the railing and leaned back, almost like she was a ballerina warming up before a recital. "Maybe you should give him a second chance."

Miranda rolled her eyes at the mere idea. "No,

thank you. Why give someone the chance to reject you twice?"

Abigail shrugged, almost as if the suggestion wasn't a big deal. "Maybe the two of you just need to talk about it. Maybe he has a good reason for not calling."

Miranda gave her a look.

"What?" Abigail lifted a shoulder. "Grant thinks highly of him, and Grant has very high standards. He wouldn't be friends with the man if he was a total jerk."

Miranda let out a sigh as she tried to consider her friend's words. "Thaddeus did help rescue me yesterday so I guess I shouldn't come down too hard on him."

Abigail held up a photo on her phone.

One that had been taken on the night of their double date back in Texas.

In the photo, Miranda and Thaddeus' heads were pressed together and both grinned as the Austin skyline sparkled behind them.

She looked . . . happy.

But that happiness had been short-lived.

Still, her heart skipped a beat as she looked at their images.

The two of them did form a striking couple.

"You guys look like you were meant to be," Abigail said as if reading her mind.

Miranda let out a self-deprecating chuckle. "I seriously doubt that. Me marrying a cowboy? You do know that's never been on my top five list of men I wouldn't mind marrying."

An astronaut had topped that list at one time, followed by a lawyer or engineer—nice stable jobs usually filled by people who were level-headed.

Abigail tilted her head, a gentle ocean breeze brushing her hair in her face and bringing with it the scent of saltwater and happier days. "No, but I do remember the Miranda who wanted to be swept off of her feet by a handsome prince."

"Are you saying that Thaddeus is a handsome prince? Is there something you haven't told me?" Miranda gave her friend a knowing look, happy to change the subject into the absurd. "Because if I have the chance to become royalty, maybe I will reconsider."

Abigail chuckled. "Well, he may not be a real-life prince. But he's definitely handsome."

Miranda agreed but didn't say anything. Instead, she scanned the beach and the road again, looking for any signs of someone watching her.

What if Brian really had followed her here?

What if he was trying to make good on his final promise: *I'll do whatever it takes to get you back.*

Only, it wasn't said sweetly. It had almost sounded more like a threat.

If that was the case, what was Miranda going to do?

The other question lingering in her head was: How was she going to glean more information about this motel and the dead body that they'd found inside? This could be just the article she needed to take her career to the next level.

At once, she remembered those papers she'd found yesterday. She'd stuffed them in her back pocket! How could she have forgotten? What if there were answers there?

She wasn't sure if there were or not.

But Miranda wanted to look at them again, just in case.

First chance she got, she needed to find them.

CHAPTER THIRTEEN

AN HOUR LATER, Thaddeus and Grant went to a restaurant called The Screen Porch Café to grab a quick lunch. To anyone watching, he may have looked relaxed, but, on the inside, Thaddeus had to fight the impulse to keep investigating.

He knew it was like Grant said—they were going to have to jump through some hoops before they recovered that dead body. But he couldn't stand the thought of that crime scene being down there and them being unable to get to it.

That also meant a killer was out there getting off scot-free, and there was nothing they could do about it.

As he glanced around the restaurant, he released some air from his lungs.

Just as the name suggested, the dining area was located on an oversized screened porch adjoining an old farmhouse on the oceanfront. The menu was handwritten on a chalkboard near the door leading to the kitchen, and the waitress was also the owner —an older woman named Mrs. Minnie, who acted like everyone's adopted grandmother.

The scent of fried fish and french fries drifted through the screens into the space along with the salty aroma of the ocean.

As he and Grant took their places at a corner table, he couldn't help but think this place felt more like gathering around grandma's kitchen table for a Thanksgiving reunion than it did a restaurant. Then again, maybe that was the point.

"Is it true what I heard last night?" a patron three tables over asked.

"There was a dead body?" someone else added.

"I remember that old motel," another man said. "I always knew it was trouble."

Thaddeus listened to each statement with curiosity. The only way he and Grant were going to find out information as to what happened there was by talking to people in this town. At least, in his experience, that was the case.

He ordered himself a crab cake sandwich, Mrs.

Minnie's specialty, along with some fries and sweet tea.

For a moment, everything felt normal.

Even though nothing was normal.

"Good afternoon, gentlemen." A man paused by their table.

Thaddeus observed him a moment. Mid-fifties, overweight, a high forehead.

"Good afternoon, Mr. Hillsdale." Grant straightened his back as if suddenly becoming more uptight. "How are you today?"

"Been better. I heard about what happened at Knobs Hill. Any leads on that dead body?"

"Not yet. We're working on it, though."

"Keep me apprised. I don't like hearing that things like this are happening in my county."

"None of us do," Grant said.

Mr. Hillsdale stepped closer and lowered his voice. "Between us, if I were you, I'd check out Winfred Preston."

"Why Winfred?" Grant asked.

"Because I saw him digging around near that sand dune not long ago."

AFTER EMMY LEFT, Abigail escaped to her room to return some calls about the wedding.

Once alone, an idea crossed Miranda's mind.

She wanted to go back to that sand dune.

This article could be the break she'd been looking for. But, first, she'd need to find more answers.

She had no intentions of going back into the motel. But she had to see it again if she wanted more information. Maybe she'd even run into Thaddeus and Grant, and she could get an update from them.

It was risky. Someone had knocked her out yesterday. She'd received threats. Been trapped in a buried motel.

Being alone might not be her best idea. But wasn't life about risks? She could be careful. Remain aware.

And the payoff could be worth it.

Before she could overthink it, she grabbed the keys to the Jeep Abigail was letting her borrow. It was Miranda's first time ever driving off-road, but she could adjust. Plus, Grant had given her a quick rundown on how to drive in the sand when he'd picked her up from the airport and drove her here.

Miranda let Abigail know she was going out for a

few minutes. Then she slipped outside and into the Jeep.

As she carefully maneuvered the vehicle, she glanced at the houses around her. This place sure was different, with its cowboys, wild horses, and isolated way of life. But it was also fascinating.

Finally, after following the path she'd walked yesterday, she reached the edge of Knobs Hill. She put the Jeep in Park and glanced around, noting that she didn't see Grant's truck. Most likely, since he was law enforcement, he'd simply driven to the spot.

However, she didn't have that privilege.

Instead, she climbed from the Jeep and began trudging across the sand dune, pulling her sweat-shirt over her hands. She hadn't worn this old sweat-shirt in years. It seemed too frumpy, too casual for her life in New York.

But, for some reason, she'd brought it with her to Cape Corral. The clothing offered some kind of strange comfort to her, and the weather today was perfect for the relaxed, teal-colored apparel.

As she crossed the sand dune, she scanned everything around her, looking for any signs of Brian. She had to be on guard. Next time, she might not be so lucky . . .

Memories of yesterday's ordeal flashed into her

mind. Those thoughts were immediately followed by a mental image of Thaddeus.

He had all the right qualities to be one of those heroes that she used to read about in romance novels. Not the trashy kind of romance novels. But the kind where heroes were actually heroes. Where chivalry existed. Where it was okay for a man to protect a woman.

That seemed to be Thaddeus.

Miranda would never tell him that to his face. But she definitely thought her words were true.

She searched the area around her, but there were no signs of Grant and Thaddeus. She thought for sure she would find them here.

But all she saw was the mound of sand known as Knobs Hill.

As Miranda walked, she tried to remain low, away from the crest of the hill where she'd be an easy target. But she couldn't walk at the base of the dune either because too much water still puddled there.

Then there was the danger of potentially falling through the sand and into the motel again. She didn't want to think it was a possibility. But anything was possible at this point.

She shuddered at the thought of it.

Finally, she reached the far side of the dune.

But there was no one out here.

She and Thaddeus had walked this far yesterday. She was sure of it.

Miranda paused and put her hands on her hips as she glanced around.

What had she missed? Why weren't Grant and Thaddeus here? And where was that opening?

Just as those questions rolled around in her mind, a figure appeared at the top of the sand dune. The sunlight lit the sky behind him, making his features indiscernible.

She clutched her throat because only one question floated in her mind . . . was that Brian?

CHAPTER FOURTEEN

THADDEUS HAD ONLY INTENDED on stopping by Knobs Hill for a few minutes. Then he'd seen the Jeep parked near the edge of the dune. Now, as he paused at the top of the ridge and glanced down, he saw the familiar figure below.

Why in the world had Miranda come back here?

Didn't she have better sense than to return here alone after everything that had happened?

He hurried down the dune toward her. But it was only when he was within spitting distance that her features softened.

She'd been afraid, hadn't she? Rightfully so after what had happened yesterday.

Thaddeus paused in front of her, caught off guard by how beautiful she looked with the sun glinting through her hair and that cozy sweatshirt on.

She wasn't his type, he reminded himself. Then why did he feel so attracted to the woman?

He cleared his throat, trying to redirect his thoughts. "What are you doing out here?"

Miranda lifted her chin. "Probably the same thing you're doing out here. I came to . . . *revisit* . . . our discovery."

He raised an eyebrow. "You were going to go back in there?"

"Not on your life would I ever go back into that space again. But I just wanted to . . ." She twisted her lips together as if she didn't know what to say.

"You wanted to snoop," he answered for her. "You hoped Grant and I would be out here, and you'd overhear something."

A flash of guilt filled her gaze. "I didn't say that."

"You didn't have to." He nodded in the direction where she'd parked. "How about if we walk back?"

"What about the motel?"

"It's gone."

Her eyes widened. "Gone?"

"I mean, it's still there. But the sand dune shifted again with the storm, and we can't find the area we fell through. Grant is trying to figure out a way to safely reach the building."

"How could a gaping hole like that just disappear?"

"That's what we're all wondering. But clearly, with Mother Nature, it's possible."

She frowned as if memories were battering her. "But there was a dead body inside . . ."

"I know. We're all well aware of that fact. Believe me."

"What are you doing out here without Grant?" Miranda's gaze narrowed with thought.

Thaddeus should have known the tables would turn so he could be more prepared with an answer. "I'm just checking things out."

"No, you were curious too. You're just as curious as I am, for that matter."

He shrugged, unable to dispute Miranda's statement. "Maybe."

"I just can't stop thinking about what happened." She ran her hands over her arms as they walked back to the parking lot.

"I know. Me neither."

They walked in silence for a few minutes. Thaddeus stole another glance at her, curious about the woman beside him. Trying to figure out who she really was.

"You still working your same job?" he tried to ask casually. "Magazine reporter, right?"

"That's right, an entertainment reporter specializing in lifestyle profiles." She said the title with a mocking accent that made it sound important. "I basically cover the rich and the famous and what their lives are like."

He raised his eyebrows before nodding. "How do you like that job?"

"It's all very interesting in a very disparaging type of way."

"Disparaging?"

"Maybe that's not the right word. I'm not exactly sure. But it's disheartening to meet people who have so much and yet they only think of themselves. I'm not saying everyone is like that. But so many have been."

"I'm sure it's eye-opening."

"Honestly, I'm highlighting the lives of those who chase a ball or sing a few tunes and make millions. I feel like I should be writing sweeping narratives about people who are fighting for human rights overseas or serving the homeless or teaching a classroom full of unruly kids who don't want to listen."

"You could always make a shift."

"I've been considering it. Especially since I arrived here and have had time to think it over. But it's taken me so long to get where I am. I just never realized how much I would hate it when I did. I've interviewed golfer Mars Jenson about his Olympic gold medal wins, Tia Louden about her ten number one pop hits, Marcus Blankenship about his hit movies. I've taken peeks into their lives. Seen their homes. Talked to their friends and employees. And it left me feeling empty instead of inspired."

"The good news is that it isn't too late for a change. You just have to want it badly enough."

She nodded. "I guess so."

Maybe that statement was directed at himself just as much as it was anyone else . . . because all he'd been thinking about since Hoffer died was the fact that he wanted to start over. That he wanted to get away from the mess at his field office and go somewhere fresh.

It wasn't that he wanted to run away from his problems . . . it was simply that being in Austin was draining every last ounce of life out of him.

How much longer until it was completely gone?

AS MIRANDA REACHED the Jeep she'd borrowed from Abigail, she spotted a white piece of paper beneath the windshield wiper.

Great. Had she not been allowed to park here? Had she just gotten a ticket of some sort?

She snatched it, glaring at the paper as if it had wronged her.

But what she saw wasn't a parking ticket.

She sucked in a quick breath before shoving the paper into her pocket.

"Is everything okay?" Thaddeus paused in front of her.

"It's fine," she said quickly.

He continued to study her face. "You don't look fine."

"I think someone's playing a joke on me. That's got to be it."

"Isn't Abigail the only one in this area who knows you? So, don't you mean that *Abigail* is playing a joke on you? I've got to say—that doesn't seem like Abigail's personality."

That's because it wasn't. But Miranda didn't say that out loud. Abigail would never do something like this to her.

But there was no one else here on the island who'd do that either.

Unless she was right, and Brian was hiding in the shadows. Maybe he'd come here to humiliate her. She wouldn't put it past him.

Still, how would he have found her? She didn't drive here, so he couldn't have followed her. Certainly, she would have noticed if he were on the plane or if he'd chartered a boat to follow her across the water to the island.

She supposed her phone could be tracked. But it had disappeared when she fell in that hole. Most likely, the sand dune had swallowed it by now.

She'd even logged onto her computer this morning to see if she could trace it.

She couldn't, which must mean it was out of service range or her battery had died.

Either way, Brian probably didn't have the resources to trace her that way.

It just didn't make sense how he would find her here.

Thaddeus stared at her another moment as if waiting for her to confess. No doubt he remembered that Emmy had said someone came looking for her at the inn. He was an FBI agent, after all.

But she wasn't going to tell him what was going on. Not now. Probably not ever.

Instead, Miranda offered a feeble smile as she

looked up at him. "I guess we should probably get back and see if the bride and groom need anything from us."

"I guess so." Even though he complied, his studious expression remained.

She pressed her lips together a moment before continuing. "However, I really think that if Grant is going to enjoy his big day, he's going to need some help finding a resolution as to what's going on here on Knobs Hill."

Thaddeus raised an eyebrow. "Are you suggesting that we investigate?"

"It seems like it's only the right thing to do, all things considered. I mean, it's practically our duty."

"You really think?"

She shrugged. "I do. You are an FBI agent, and I am a reporter . . . it only makes sense."

Thaddeus remained silent a moment.

Miranda held her breath as she waited to hear what he would say. Though part of her wanted to avoid the man at all costs, his experience and credentials would be an asset.

She just had no idea if he felt the same way.

CHAPTER FIFTEEN

AS THADDEUS CLIMBED BACK into the truck Grant had let him borrow, his suspicions continued to rise.

He'd gotten a brief glimpse of whatever had been left on Miranda's windshield.

It had been a picture of a slightly overweight brunette with glasses.

Why would someone leave a picture like that on Miranda's car?

It didn't make sense. But he hadn't pushed the issue. It wasn't his business.

However, leaving the photo didn't seem like something Abigail would do. Thaddeus didn't know his friend's fiancée *that* well, but Abigail seemed way too sensible to drive all the way out here to leave a random picture on a windshield.

He suspected his initial theory was correct.

Miranda was hiding something.

Something that went deeper than whatever had happened yesterday—both when she was attacked and when they were trapped in that motel. Maybe she'd even come to Cape Corral to escape from something.

Thaddeus wasn't judging her for that. Maybe he'd come here to escape from his problems as well. He still hadn't gotten over watching his partner die in front of him and the betrayal that followed.

He shoved the memories aside as he twisted the key to start the truck, but the engine wouldn't turn over.

Thaddeus tried again but nothing happened.

He groaned. The last thing he needed was to be stuck here again.

As he popped the hood and climbed out, he motioned for Miranda to wait for him.

But before he could check out the engine, his phone rang. It was Grant.

"We have a theory on the body."

"Based on the tattoo sketch I gave you?" Had to

be. As far as he knew, the body still hadn't been recovered.

"Yes, I'll tell you more details when I see you."

"Where are you?" Thaddeus raised the hood, latched it open and stared at the engine, trying to figure out what was wrong.

"I'm heading to Abigail's. Can you meet me there?"

He frowned when he saw the spark plug wires had been cut. "It looks like someone tampered with your truck engine out by Knobs Hill."

"What? I can come out and give you a ride."

He glanced at Miranda who still sat in the Jeep staring at him in curiosity. "I can get a ride with Miranda. But you'll need to send someone out here to look at this."

"Will do."

As he ended the call, Thaddeus quickly motioned to Miranda again.

She rolled down her window. "Car trouble?"

"Yes, but there's more. Grant thinks he knows who that body belongs to."

Her eyebrows scrunched together. "How?"

"The guy had a snake tattoo."

"You can ID someone just from their tattoo?"

"Sometimes. Tattoo recognition technology is a

useful tool law enforcement can use to match a tattoo with a particular person. We're going to meet at Abigail's to talk about what he found out."

Something flickered in her gaze. Curiosity? Maybe.

Maybe something more.

Thaddeus slammed the hood shut and strode across the sand toward her. "Mind giving me a ride?"

"Hop in." She nodded toward the passenger seat.

"Do you think Grant would let me hear the update?" she asked as he climbed in.

"You'd have to ask him when we get there." But as he strapped on his seatbelt, he realized he felt nervous.

Nervous? About riding with Miranda?

Certainly, the woman was a capable driver.

For some reason, he still felt more apprehensive than he should.

———

MIRANDA COULDN'T STOP THINKING about that photo.

The one of the unassuming, overweight girl with dark hair and glasses.

A photo of *her*.

From six years ago.

In the time since then, she'd remade herself into a new person. A successful person. Someone worthy of doing stories on the rich and famous. Who fit into New York society and blended in with her uppity counterparts.

The reinvention had been a turning point in her career, one that had allowed her to get her dream job with *Paragon* magazine.

Though it wasn't a fashion magazine, the whole media was steeped in image. They hadn't wanted to hire someone mousy who didn't care about fashion.

So she'd had a makeover. Gotten a new wardrobe. Tapped into a more outgoing side of herself while forgoing any mentions of the side of her that liked *The Lord of the Rings* or Narnia or Harry Potter.

She was a little more than seven months in, and the job seemed to consume her entire life.

But it was what she'd always wanted to do. How could she complain now that she had what she'd always desired?

Since she was a child, she'd only wanted to work as a reporter in New York. She'd just had no idea she'd have to sacrifice her true self to do so.

No, not her true self. The way she dressed and

lived . . . those were just outward things. Who she was on the inside was a quiet girl who loved reading and nights at home. That hadn't changed. She still loved those things.

She just had to suppress that introverted side of her while on the job.

But it was also a part of her past that she tried to bury. When she thought about how she used to dress and fix her hair . . . it was embarrassing, especially considering the people that she was around in New York. They would never understand.

Of course, Abigail knew her that way and had loved Miranda when she was heavy, and she'd loved Miranda when she was thin. It was one of the reasons Miranda considered Abigail such a close friend now.

But, still, Miranda didn't want others to know.

She definitely didn't want Thaddeus to see her picture—not that she wanted to impress him or anything of that sort.

Miranda wasn't sure why insecurity still gripped her at times. But it did. Whether it was right or wrong, it was the truth.

As she tried to shift while driving on the sand, her back tires turned in place.

"Don't press too hard." Thaddeus leaned closer

and pointed to the floorboards. "Ease up on the accelerator some."

Miranda's heartrate quickened at Thaddeus' closeness. She swallowed hard, determined to ignore the feeling and to get Thaddeus Blackwell out of her blood. Instead, she did as he said and slowly climbed from the hole her tires had dug.

She let out a breath. She was a little on edge, wasn't she? Thaddeus being with her now was a good thing, even if it was difficult being around him.

"Why don't you try to drive on the beach side of the dunes?" he suggested. "Grant said the sand is more packed there."

"Now that you mention it, Grant did say something about that to me as well."

"It can't hurt to give it a try."

As soon as Miranda found a road that crossed over, she left the residential side of the island where houses were nestled between dunes and went onto the beach side.

She rolled down her window and the breath left her lungs with exhilaration as she found herself riding beside the Atlantic with the wind in her hair.

"This seems like a once-in-a-lifetime thing." She drew in a deep breath as adrenaline pumped through her. "This is amazing."

"This whole place seems like a parallel universe."

She stole a glance at Thaddeus—at his strong, handsome profile—before glancing back at the beach around them. They were the only ones out here. At this very moment, she felt like they had this whole island to themselves.

"You're right," she murmured. "It is. It's the real Upside Down."

He stole a glance at her. "Now you're using *Stranger Things* references?"

"You inspired me." She grinned. "But, really, this place seems like the polar opposite of New York. I can move and breathe and think."

"If you don't like New York, why do you live there?"

She shrugged, not expecting his question. "Because it's where my job is."

He didn't say anything.

But she turned the thought over in her mind as she continued down the beach.

Why *did* she stay in New York? She thought she would love living there, but instead the fast-paced, crowded city gave her anxiety.

Yet she'd latched onto the assumption that she wouldn't be able to work anywhere else.

However, there were writing jobs she could do

other places. People worked from home all the time. Her job required so much travel anyway . . .

But her editor, Helena, insisted that her staff writers live in the city and work in the office.

The woman practically reminded Miranda of Meryl Streep in *The Devil Wears Prada*.

She sighed, the thoughts weighing on her mind. They had been there for a while, but now that she was away from New York, she felt like she could see things more clearly. She'd been so busy at her new job that she didn't have much time to think or reflect.

A few moments later, a dark vehicle appeared in her rearview mirror. She watched it a moment, noting how the driver quickly gained on them.

Miranda tensed as the vehicle remained behind her, even though the wide expanse of beach would allow him to easily pass.

"What's wrong?" Thaddeus asked.

There he went again, sensing Miranda's every thought even when she tried to hide them.

"The truck behind me is making me nervous," she admitted.

He glanced over his shoulder. "You just keep driving like you are, and he'll go around you if he wants to pass. This is probably where a lot of the locals drive."

She nodded and gripped the steering wheel tighter. Thaddeus' words made sense. She'd already noticed that many drivers tried to follow the furrows left by the tires of vehicles who'd gone before them.

But the next instant, she felt a nudge.

The truck had hit her bumper.

"Thaddeus!" she screamed.

Before he could say anything, the driver rammed her again. This time, he clipped her back bumper at an angle.

She lost control and the Jeep careened toward the sand dune.

As it did, her left two tires went airborne.

Then everything turned upside down.

CHAPTER SIXTEEN

WHEN THE JEEP STOPPED ROLLING, Thaddeus glanced beside him.

Miranda hung upside down, her hair cascading onto the ceiling.

But she blinked.

She was alive! Thank God . . .

"Are you okay?" he rushed, examining Miranda again.

She touched the side of her head. She had a small cut there. "I don't know. I think so."

He quickly glanced behind them and saw the truck speeding off.

Whoever had done this had done so on purpose.

"We need to get you out of here." He smelled

gasoline in the air. They couldn't take any chances or waste any time right now.

"Okay . . ." But she squeezed her eyes closed as if in discomfort.

"I'm going to unbuckle your seatbelt. I'll do my best to catch you when it releases. I don't want you falling and hitting your head. Can you use your arms to help support yourself?" He asked the question even though he knew Miranda had no choice at this point.

"I think so." Her eyes fluttered open, but her gaze still looked glazed, as if she were still in shock over everything.

Carefully, Thaddeus reached for his own seatbelt. He braced his hands on the ceiling of the Jeep to break his fall. Once he'd lowered himself, he reached for Miranda.

"I'm going to catch you, okay?" he murmured.

"Okay." Her voice wavered as she said the word.

He reached for her buckle and pressed the button. As Miranda started to fall, he scooted over so he was beneath her. Thankfully, she didn't have that far to drop.

She let out a little moan as her body collided with his.

Obviously, something hurt from their crash.

But the smell of gas reminded Thaddeus they needed to move faster.

"Can you crawl out that window?" He nodded beside her, glad she'd had the window rolled down.

"I'll do my best." Miranda winced as she turned and began to crawl.

He kept a hand on her back, silently encouraging her to move more quickly.

Finally, she was out of the Jeep and nearly collapsed onto the sand on the other side.

Thaddeus crawled out behind her and quickly stood, helping her to her feet.

He then took her hand and pulled her away from the scene, moving as quickly as possible.

He was just in time.

The next instant, an explosion filled the air.

The Jeep went up in flames.

"WE HAVE a small clinic here on the island," Grant explained as he stood in front of Miranda at the accident scene. "Let me have the doctor check you out—"

"I'll be fine." Miranda held a clean cloth over the

cut on her forehead and winced. "I promise. I'm just a little bruised and shaken."

Thaddeus' jaw visibly tightened as he stood beside Grant. "You could have died."

Miranda didn't need reminding. Every time she closed her eyes, the crash filled her thoughts.

"You could have died too," she reminded him.

Thaddeus stood with his hands on his hips as he watched Miranda's every move, almost as if he felt personally responsible for her health and safety.

Thank goodness he'd encouraged her to get out of the Jeep when he did. Miranda had been so stunned she'd only wanted to sit there. If Miranda had wasted any more time, she would have been in the Jeep when the explosion occurred.

They both would have been.

A shiver raced through her at the thought.

She sat on the tailgate of Grant's forestry truck as another officer examined the Jeep. The fire chief, someone named Dillion McGrath, was also on the scene.

Miranda wanted nothing more than to make Grant and Abigail's big day special and stress-free. Yet she felt like all she'd done since arriving was to cause more trouble—without even trying to.

"I'm so sorry about Abigail's Jeep, Grant," Miranda started.

"It's not your fault. She'll understand. Vehicles can be replaced. People can't."

Miranda nodded, although she still felt responsible.

The moments before the crash replayed in her mind. She pictured that black truck behind them.

Who had been behind the wheel? Brian?

Or did this have something to do with the dead body she and Thaddeus had found in the old motel?

Miranda didn't know. Neither thought comforted her, especially when she realized that somebody clearly wanted her dead.

This person had come awfully close to succeeding.

She was sure Grant and his guys would be on the lookout for that truck. Would they find it? On an island without any usable bridges, it would be hard to get the vehicle away. Still, there seemed to be a lot of places to hide here on the island.

"Since you're both here, I thought I'd tell you that we think we know the identity of the man you found in the Sand Spur," Grant said. "It's based purely on the tattoo, and it's only a theory."

"Who?" Miranda asked, even though she realized she probably wouldn't know who the man was.

"Someone named Bobby Joe Taylor. He works for a company that installs security systems at businesses up and down the East Coast. He went missing two days ago."

"Is he from around here?" Thaddeus asked.

"A town called Elizabeth City, which isn't too far away. Anyway, we're still looking into it. I hope we'll get the permit so we can begin excavating the site soon."

"Thanks for the update." Thaddeus glanced back at her, his eyes still full of concern as he turned to address her. "Maybe we should get you back to the house."

His care for her touched Miranda more than she thought it would.

Brian? He would have probably gotten out of the Jeep and run away, without even bothering to help her escape.

Just like he'd done when the drugstore had been robbed and the two of them had been inside.

Miranda still shuddered at the thought. At the memory that someone she'd cared about had abandoned her when she needed him most.

She stood and glanced at Grant, her body sore

and achy. "If it's okay, I would like to get back and rest."

"Of course. I'm going to need to stay here and investigate a little bit longer." Grant grabbed something from his truck. "By the way, the timing might seem wrong, but I got a new phone for you since you lost yours."

"Thank you so much," Miranda told him. She needed to call Helena and check in.

On second thought, maybe she'd been better off without a phone . . .

Grant glanced at Thaddeus. "But I don't want Miranda left alone right now. Not until we know what's happening."

"My thoughts exactly. I'll keep an eye on her."

"I don't need a babysitter." Miranda bristled. They were talking as if she couldn't hear them.

Thaddeus locked gazes with her. "Then think of me as your personal bodyguard."

CHAPTER SEVENTEEN

THADDEUS AND MIRANDA caught a ride back to Abigail's house with Officer Fulton.

Grant hadn't needed to tell Thaddeus to stay with Miranda because he'd planned on doing that anyway. After what had happened, they couldn't take any chances.

But he needed to get to the bottom of what was going on with her. Sure, the hit-and-run explosion was most likely tied with the dead body they'd found. But he'd like to speak to her about it. There was more going on with her than she was letting on. He was certain of it.

Once they were inside Abigail's house, he glanced around.

Grant had mentioned something about Abigail going down to the station to help with the horses. He welcomed the privacy right now.

Thaddeus turned to Miranda. "We need to talk."

Miranda didn't argue. Instead, she followed him to the couch in the living room. She sat on one end and he on the other.

He leaned forward and locked his gaze with hers. "Is there anything at all that you need to tell me?"

She pressed her lips together as if contemplating what to say.

Finally, she let out a long breath. "I hadn't wanted to get into this. But I don't really have much choice now, do I?"

"I'm listening," Thaddeus prodded.

"About two months ago, I broke up with a man named Brian Bowers. It wasn't a good breakup, and one of the last things he said to me was that he was going to do anything he could to win me back."

"And, by that, do you think he followed you here and is stalking you?"

Her expression became even more pinched. "I don't know. I mean, I received some strange threats before I came. Once I got here, I thought I saw someone staring at me outside the house. I couldn't make out any details, so I don't know who it was. I just don't see how he would have found me."

A frown tugged at his lips. "Did this Brian guy ever show any signs of being dangerous?"

Miranda let out a sigh. "He was very passionate, if that makes sense. He had strong opinions on everything. Maybe even some control issues. Do those things equal dangerous? Not necessarily. But possibly."

Thaddeus leaned back, trying not to appear as if he were interrogating her. "Do you mind if I ask what happened?"

Her face seemed to go paler as she only stared at him. Her gaze appeared strained and uncertain.

"How about if I grab you some water first?" Thaddeus asked, figuring she might need a moment to collect herself.

Before Miranda could confirm that she wanted any, he rose and grabbed her a glass. After handing it to her and making sure she took a few sips, he sat back down—beside her this time.

Miranda rubbed her throat as she took another moment to compose herself. "Just to give you a little history . . . we met when I was eating with a friend outside at a restaurant. He said he saw me from across the street, and I was the most beautiful woman he'd ever seen. He asked me out."

"And you said yes?"

"Initially, I said no. But I did give him my phone number. He called me that night, and we talked. In fact, he called me every night for the next week until I agreed to meet him."

"What does this guy do for a living?"

"He works in finance." She took a long sip of water. "Anyway, we met for dinner and had a good time. He made me feel like a million bucks. Part of me kept reminding myself about the Bible verse that says charm is deceptive. But I wanted to believe he was the real thing. His attention . . . it really was flattering."

"It sounds like you liked him."

She shrugged. "I didn't dislike him. Although, I had many moments I thought about calling it off, my roommate insisted that I should give him a shot instead of dismissing him so easily. She said I was acting judgmental."

"Why would she say that?"

Miranda rubbed her throat as if she didn't want to share. Finally, she shrugged again. "She thought I was too picky. That I liked ideals. That I would be a fool not to go out with Brian. On the surface, he seemed   perfect.   Handsome,   successful, charismatic."

"I take it there's a *but* in there . . ."

"About two months ago, Brian and I were out on a date. On the way home, we ran into a drugstore to pick up something and . . ." She blew out a breath. "Anyway, while we were inside, two gunmen entered the store."

Thaddeus tensed as he waited to hear how the story would play out.

"As soon as Brian saw the gunmen, he fled. He left me in the store to face those men alone. He didn't even look back." Her voice cracked.

Thaddeus' spine tightened at the thought. How could any man do that?

"I know that people sometimes react in unex-pected ways in situations like those—"

"Don't make excuses for him."

Her gaze fluttered to meet his. "I know I shouldn't. And I try not to. That night, he showed me what I already knew—that he cared only about himself."

The thought of someone leaving Miranda in a situation like that made another surge of anger race through Thaddeus' blood. "What happened after that?"

She rubbed her throat again. "One of the gunmen grabbed me. Put the gun to my head. Told the cashier if he didn't empty the drawer that he'd shoot me."

"You must have been terrified."

"To say the least. I thought I was going to die. I really did." Miranda drew in another deep breath. "But, thankfully, the cashier did as the man said and gave him the money. Then this guy must have heard police cars in the distance because he and his buddy ran, leaving me unharmed—physically, at least."

"I can imagine." He knew exactly what she was saying.

The emotional scars were still there.

No wonder she'd looked so terrified when Thaddeus had climbed out of the motel first. She'd been afraid he would leave her behind, hadn't she?

She needn't have worried. He wouldn't do that to a stranger, much less someone he cared about.

More tension pulled taut across his chest.

If he knew what was good for him, he wouldn't allow himself to care about her. But he was finding it more and more difficult not to.

"What did Brian say when he finally saw you again?"

"He acted like he was so happy that I was okay. He apologized. But I knew at that point that we couldn't be together. The relationship already had warning signs of being toxic. I should have broken up with him earlier, but I was trying to be more open-minded."

"He didn't handle the breakup well?"

"No. I don't think Brian is used to not getting his way. He tried to shower me with gifts in an effort to win me back. But I was done."

Thaddeus reached forward and squeezed her hand. "I'm sorry, Miranda. You deserve better than that."

Her cheeks reddened as she glanced up at him. "Thank you."

He suddenly realized what he'd done and pulled his hand away. He'd had no intentions of touching her. He'd had no intentions of *liking* her.

But he'd be lying if he denied that something was beginning to change inside him. When he'd first seen Miranda again, all he'd felt was irritation and anger. That had morphed into confusion.

Much of that confusion was still there.

But a deep desire to continue getting to know this woman still remained.

And it wasn't going anywhere anytime soon.

The bad news was that Thaddeus had no idea what to do about it.

Because having his heart broken again by someone he thought he could trust just might be the end of him.

MIRANDA TOOK another sip of her water and leaned back into the couch.

Even though she hadn't intended to share all that with Thaddeus, getting that story about Brian off her chest had felt good. She'd tried to tell her roommate —a woman who was her polar opposite—about it, but Tanya had thought she was crazy to turn Brian away afterward.

Tanya had the uncanny ability to constantly make Miranda doubt herself. Gaslighting was one of the woman's many talents. But Tanya had also been the one who'd helped Miranda with her makeover, who'd helped transform her from bookworm into a successful entertainer reporter.

Miranda let out a sigh and turned her thoughts back to her conversation with Thaddeus.

He'd been a surprisingly good listener.

Or was he using his FBI skills to get information out of her?

Miranda's feelings about the man continued to be all over the place.

Was he the sweet, charming man she'd met back in Austin?

Or was he the jerk face who'd kissed her and never called again?

Miranda wasn't sure. She wanted to believe he was the kind, compassionate man in front of her now.

But she couldn't afford to make any mistakes again.

Not after Brian.

Her muscles still trembled after the earlier incident in the Jeep. That had been close. She was so glad Thaddeus was there or she wouldn't have made it out of the situation alive.

The man had saved her life not once but twice now.

"Listen, if it's okay, I'm going to go take a quick shower." She quickly stood.

He rushed to his feet also. "Of course."

They stood in front of each other, entirely too close. As they did, Miranda stared up into his eyes.

His beautiful, warm brown eyes.

At once, her thoughts went back to the kiss they'd shared the night they met. To the connection she'd felt with him. To the hope he'd ignited inside her.

She licked her lips as she imagined kissing him again.

Then her heartbreak came rushing back, reminding her to keep her distance, and she stepped back instead.

"I'll only be a few minutes," she said.

Thaddeus rubbed his jaw and averted his gaze a moment, as if his thoughts had drifted back in time also. "Of course. Take your time."

But, as she slipped into the bathroom, she pulled out her phone and quickly set it up.

She was going to look into Brian. Call a few of their mutual friends. See if she could find out where he was.

Because whatever was going on needed to stop.

Could Brian have been responsible for what happened?

She didn't know.

The only thing she could think about was the fact that she needed to write this story.

Then she needed to get a job outside of New York City so she could get away from the lures that had trapped her there. She'd thought everything she wanted could be found in the city. Her dream job. Her future. Her identity.

She'd been wrong. So, so wrong.

Why had it taken her so long to see it?

CHAPTER EIGHTEEN

THADDEUS TRIED to put any thoughts about Miranda out of his head.

How could one woman get under his skin so badly?

He had no idea.

But as she'd stood in front of him and he'd remembered everything that transpired between them, he'd wanted nothing more than to pull her into his arms.

Thank goodness, she'd stepped back before he made that mistake again.

As soon as she emerged from the shower, he had a proposition for her.

"I want to go check out the accident scene," he announced.

Her eyes lit with surprise. "Right now?"

He nodded. "I want to see if there are any updates. Are you okay with that?"

She didn't have to think about it long before nodding. "I'm more than okay with it. I'm feeling a little better now after taking a shower. I'd like to see what's going on also."

"Great. Let's go."

They walked together toward the scene. He hoped he didn't regret this.

He was going to keep an eye out for any signs of trouble.

When they approached, Grant was still at the scene, along with Officer Fulton and the fire chief.

"Anything?" Thaddeus asked as he joined them and watched as a tow truck pulled the Jeep out of the sand.

"No." Grant frowned, his gaze fastened on Thaddeus. "I'm afraid not. We've questioned several people, but no one saw anything. As soon as we clear the area, we'll begin searching the island for any sign of that black truck. But, as strange as it may sound, even though the island is small, it can still be difficult to locate vehicles in situations like this."

"I understand. If someone doesn't want to be

found, then they'll put up plenty of obstacles to ensure they're not."

"You didn't have to come back out, you know." Grant glanced at Miranda and then observed Thaddeus for a moment as if trying to read his thoughts.

Thaddeus shrugged as he contemplated his answer. "You know I'm not good at sitting back and doing nothing. We both wanted to see what's going on with this."

Grant's gaze locked in on Miranda. "How are you doing?"

"Shaken but hanging in." She stared at the Jeep's blackened remains, visibly shuddering as if she were mentally reliving what had happened.

Thaddeus shoved down the sudden urge to wrap an arm around her waist for support. If he didn't stop having these inclinations, he was going to be in trouble sooner rather than later.

"That's good to hear." Grant nodded.

Thaddeus glanced at the Jeep again before looking at Grant. "What do you know about Winfred Preston?"

"Winfred? Are you still thinking about what Hillsdale said?"

Thaddeus ran a hand through his hair. "Maybe. Someone is clearly targeting Miranda, and maybe me too. Someone wants to keep us quiet. I just want to explore every possibility right now."

Grant let out a breath as he seemed to think through Thaddeus' question. "There's not much to say about Winfred. He's a little eccentric. Lives by himself. A confirmed bachelor for years. But he's never really been in any trouble. When I went by to check him out, he wasn't home."

"Where can I find this guy?"

Grant rattled off his address. "It's within walking distance from here."

"If you don't mind, I think I'm going to go pay him a visit," Thaddeus announced. "I may talk to Hillsdale again also so I can get more information on what he saw."

"Is this in an official capacity? Or are you still on a leave of absence?"

"I just started back to work a few weeks ago. But this isn't official. It's personal."

"I understand. Knock yourself out," Grant said. "Just be careful. Until we know what's going on, we all need to be careful."

Thaddeus couldn't agree more.

MIRANDA'S THOUGHTS raced as she thought about the conversation Thaddeus was having with Grant.

Leave of absence?

What was that about?

Before she could say anything, he turned toward her and took her elbow. "Care to take a walk?"

He was actually going to invite her to go with him to talk to both Hillsdale and this Winfred guy?

Miranda wasn't going to argue about that.

"Sounds good." She waited until they were away from Grant before asking, "Who are Hillsdale and Winfred?"

He filled her in on the men, explaining that Hillsdale had once been the county superintendent who'd approved that motel when any other propositions had been rejected. He then explained that Winfred had been spotted digging holes on Knobs Hill."

"You didn't think to mention that to me earlier?" She paused and her hands went to her hips.

Thaddeus scowled. "I was afraid you might come out by yourself to question people. It's not a good idea, Miranda. Whoever is involved with this is dangerous."

"I need some answers."

"Why?"

"I want to write an article on this motel buried under Knobs Hill. It's just the kind of feature piece that might land me another job, one not with *Paragon* and one not in New York City."

He stared at her another moment. "I know you indicated you weren't entirely happy there. But I didn't know you wanted to leave."

"It's . . . it's not everything it's cracked up to be."

"I see." He paused, as if waiting to see if she'd disclose more.

But she didn't want to focus on that now. She had to get the story written first. "Are you sure you're okay about us working together on this? We have to work together on the wedding, but this . . . adds a whole other dimension."

Thaddeus stared at her, thoughts swirling in his gaze, before he finally nodded. "I like to think of myself as a man of my word."

She stared at him, remembering how he'd never called her.

But maybe she needed to let that go for a minute.

"Okay then. Let's do this."

CHAPTER NINETEEN

THADDEUS FIGURED it was better if he was with Miranda when she asked these questions than if she was alone. His gut told him she would be investigating this with or without him.

But he still couldn't help but feel guarded, especially after everything that had happened. They could have been killed—not once but twice.

Until they had more answers, he had no idea if whoever tried to kill them would come after them again.

His best guess was that they would.

"So . . . I'm glad you weren't hurt earlier." Miranda meandered down the road with her hands in the pockets of her well-worn jeans.

Thaddeus remained beside her, images of their date flashing in his mind. They'd meandered then too . . . even when it had started raining, they'd kept walking and talking and laughing.

That was the moment he'd known Miranda was special.

"I'm glad you weren't hurt either," he finally said.

She paused on the road and turned toward him, her gaze turning serious. "In order to work together on this and the wedding . . . we have to put the past behind us."

He swallowed hard, wondering where she was going with this. "Yes, we do. I would hate for anything to ruin Grant's big day."

"So, maybe we should just pretend that our date never happened." Miranda's gaze locked with his even as her voice sounded strained. "We just have to accept that things didn't work out between us and move on."

A lump formed in his throat. Moving on was the last thing he wanted to do.

Actually, it was exactly what he knew he should do.

But his heart said otherwise.

And every time he looked at her lips . . . he imagined that kiss they'd shared as the rain drenched them and an acoustic band played "Brown Eyed Girl" at a nearby bar.

There had been something so unassuming about Miranda . . . and he'd found that quality extremely attractive. He'd found everything about her attractive. And the connection they'd shared . . .

He pulled his thoughts back to the present. "We should do that for Grant and Abigail's sake."

"Exactly." She nodded, but her gaze looked jumbled with emotions.

Or was that just wishful thinking?

Another part of him wanted to confront her. He wanted to hear her explanation as to how she'd had such a brisk change so soon after their time together.

But they'd had only one date. It wasn't like they had a long history behind them. Miranda had no obligation to explain herself.

Besides, she was right. It was best if neither of them dwelled on their botched relationship anymore. They needed to put what had happened behind them and keep looking forward.

"What exactly are you going to ask Hillsdale?" Miranda asked, easily moving on to another subject.

"I'm not sure yet. But I smell something dirty. Maybe he knows something."

"I'm not sure what I'm going to ask him either."

"You think he's going to tell you something that he won't tell me?" Thaddeus raised an eyebrow.

"Maybe. I *am* less intimidating."

"You don't think he's just going to outright tell you whatever you need to know, do you?" Thaddeus listened closely, sincerely curious about what she would say.

Miranda turned toward him, something flashing in her gaze. Irritation? Maybe.

"I may not be an FBI agent, but I *am* capable of finding out answers. I know you think I just write little profile pieces, but I always aim to go deeper than just surface information on these celebrities. I talk to friends from these people's childhood. I talk to neighbors, coworkers. I find out what they were like before success."

"Understood. I wasn't—"

"And you know what?" she continued. "None of them seem happier now that they're successful."

"Is that right?"

"Money has only added to their problems in most cases." Her words contained a certain wistfulness that he wanted to understand more.

But that would have to wait until later.

"I wasn't trying to imply you weren't capable. But

the kind of questions you're used to asking probably don't put you in danger. That's what I worry about."

She tucked her hands into the sleeves of her sweatshirt and shrugged. "I appreciate your concern, but I can look out for myself."

Thaddeus started to say something, but he closed his mouth. He wanted to bring up the fact that Miranda hadn't done a great job looking out for herself yesterday. Or today.

But he had a feeling she wouldn't handle that kind of statement very well.

"Here's where Hillsdale lives." Thaddeus glanced at his phone to confirm the address before nodding toward a white house in the distance. "You ready for this?"

"Absolutely."

Thaddeus dragged in a deep breath and prayed this would go more smoothly than their earlier efforts.

———

"WELL, if it isn't Grant's friend. Thaddeus, right?" Hillsdale stood outside his house in front of a wood smoker.

The scent of hickory-smoked barbecued pork floated in the air and made Miranda's stomach rumble.

"That's right," Thaddeus said. "This is my friend, Miranda."

She smiled at him as they shook hands.

"Pleasure to meet you," he said. "Don't mind me. I'm smoking my famous pork barbecue for a fundraiser for the wild horse fund. Do it every year. You'll have to try some before you leave Cape Corral. I've won top honors at the island's cookoff for five years straight now."

"It smells wonderful," Miranda said, noting how the man said everything with flourish and grandiose, as if he were the most important person around.

He placed his tongs in a holder on the smoker and turned to them. "So, to what do I owe this visit?"

"We were hoping to ask you a few questions." Miranda tried to keep her voice unassuming.

She'd been thinking about her strategy the whole way here and had decided she shouldn't be too pushy. She would employ a gentle approach first to see if she could get answers.

"Questions?" His eyebrows shot in the air. "I can only assume you're talking about the motel."

"That's right," Miranda said. "Do you mind if we have a few minutes of your time?"

"Of course." Hillsdale stretched his arm behind him, inviting them to sit on some nearby patio chairs.

Miranda looked around a moment. She was glad Thaddeus was with her. Even though she tried to sound strong and sure of herself, some self-doubt still nagged at the back of her mind.

Someone had tried to kill her, and she needed to keep that fact in mind. Especially being out in the open like this.

After they settled into the cushioned seats, Hillsdale sat in a chair across from them.

"Now what do you want to know? I've already told you about Winfred. Have you questioned him yet?"

"No, we haven't," Thaddeus interjected. "Grant stopped by his place, but apparently, Winfred wasn't home. Grant is obviously the one officially investigating this."

"Exactly. Which is why I'm curious why the two of you are here right now." He raised an eyebrow, not bothering to hide his scrutiny.

"We don't mean any harm," Miranda said. "I'm just terribly curious about this old motel. In fact, I'm a reporter with *Paragon* magazine in New York. You may have heard of it. I thought this could be a fascinating piece on the area. In fact, the mention might even bring in some more tourism."

The man's eyes lit.

Bingo. That was his currency.

Tourism.

Because tourism would bring more people, which would result in more tax dollars for the county. That was exactly what someone in Hillsdale's position usually wanted, at least in Miranda's experience.

"I think an article sounds like a very interesting idea." His eyes flashed as if he saw an opportunity ahead. "I'd be more than happy to accommodate."

This man was such a politician.

"Do you have any old pictures of the motel?" Miranda started.

"As a matter of fact, I do. As I'm sure you've heard, the place was very controversial when it was built."

"I heard you were a huge proponent for having it built, despite the protests of the community." Miranda kept her voice firm but kind.

"Sometimes, people in the community can't see the entire picture like I do. Everyone always looks after their own interests first. Change can be hard to come by."

"And what is that entire picture?" Thaddeus asked.

Hillsdale stood, picked up the tongs and prodded the wood inside the smoker as if buying time. Finally, he raised his tongs in the air and pointed at the two of them as if to drive home his point. "It goes back to tourism again. I want to protect this island, but I also know that we need money in order to do so. So, in my mind, having one motel on this island was a win-win. It's not like we have anything else here, like fast food restaurants or chain stores. A locally owned motel seemed like a good compromise."

"You said locally owned?" Miranda repeated. "Who owned it?"

"Several people in the community invested in it."

Now that was an interesting statement. Before she had a chance to ask about it, Thaddeus jumped in.

"Did someone act as the managing owner?" he asked.

"Yes, a man named Alexander Gavin. But he passed away a couple of years ago."

That lead fizzled before it ever had time to

develop . . . but she wasn't done with her questions yet.

"No one ever looked into demolishing the motel before the sand covered it?" Miranda continued.

Hillsdale shrugged. "Shifting sand is just a part of life on the islands. That hotel's not the only thing buried around here. There's an entire mini golf course covered by Jockey's Ridge down in Nags Head. There's also an old motel underneath that sand dune, dating back to the time when Jockey's Ridge was actually used to watch horse races. Besides, Knobs Hill is protected, and safety inspectors determined the motel wasn't going to be a nuisance to people on the island." He shrugged again. "It looks like they were wrong."

"Have any other people here on the island ever had any mishaps with the place?" Miranda asked.

"Not that I've heard of. Once it was gone and buried, it was pretty much gone and buried. People moved on. On an island like this, people have to work hard for a living. They're busy with charter fishing or running their rental business or doing whatever it takes to earn a living."

Miranda continued taking mental notes. "I understand."

"The one other person I think you might want to talk to is Jared Durbin. He used to live at the motel, and he was furious when he heard the county was closing it due to the encroaching sand. In fact, he chained himself to a post out front once in protest."

"You think he could have something to do with this?" Thaddeus asked.

"He had a strange attachment to the place. That's all I'm saying."

"Thank you for the information," Miranda said. "And, just to clarify, to your knowledge there are no other openings to get into this motel? The whole thing is completely buried?"

He quirked an eyebrow. "That's correct. Why? Do you think otherwise?"

"I'm just asking questions," Miranda said.

Thaddeus suddenly stood beside her, his hand on her elbow as he tugged her up beside him. "This has really been so helpful. Thank you for your time, Mr. Hillsdale."

Why was he ushering her away so quickly? Did he know something that she didn't?

"I may have more questions later," Miranda quickly told Hillsdale.

"Of course. Whatever you need to know, you can

come back to me. I'd be more than happy to share anything that I know."

Before Miranda could say anything else, Thaddeus led her away.

CHAPTER TWENTY

"WHAT WAS THAT ABOUT?" Miranda demanded as soon as they were out of earshot.

Thaddeus shrugged. "You have to know when to ask questions and know when to back off."

"Why would you say that?"

"He was getting suspicious about your line of questioning."

"How do you know? He seemed fine to me."

"I've been trained on doing interrogations and have more than a decade of experience with it. I'd like to think I'm pretty good at reading people." Even as Thaddeus said the words, part of him knew that wasn't entirely true. He'd questioned himself more than he should lately.

Especially after what happened with Hoffer.

Miranda stared at him a moment. As she did, the sinking sun turned the sky various hues of pink.

It was quite the sight . . . Miranda and the sunset made for one beautiful picture.

"Okay. I'll trust you on this," she said in a near whisper, as if her walls were beginning to crumble.

He came close to kissing her right then and there.

But he stopped himself just before leaning in. If he allowed himself to do that, he'd be helpless to resist her from here on out.

Instead, he cleared his thoughts and nodded to a house in the distance. "If I understand the directions Grant gave me, Winfred's house should be right over there. We should see if we can talk to him while we're out." Thaddeus paused before clarifying, "For your article."

"Exactly. For my article."

The two of them began walking down the sandy road. Several minutes later, they veered from the main street cutting through the island and onto one of the smaller ones leading toward the woods. They stopped at an unkempt bungalow.

Thaddeus knocked at the door, but he heard

only silence in return. No movement. No curtains being shoved to the side.

Nothing.

"I don't think he's home," Thaddeus told Miranda.

Miranda frowned. "That's how it appears, doesn't it?"

"No telling how long he'll be out. It's getting late, and it's been a long day. You're going to be sore in the morning. So am I. What do you say the two of us get back?"

"I just feel like we've been out here searching for answers all day, and we haven't found anything. We don't even have any good suspects."

"There's Mr. Hillsdale. Winfred. Brian?"

She frowned as if unsatisfied. "I know that Grant and Abigail plan to go down to the courthouse tomorrow to pick up their wedding license. Maybe while they're out the two of us will have a chance to look into this some more. After that, the rest of the wedding party will be coming into town, and I know things are going to get even crazier."

"In other words, we don't have much time if we want to figure out what's going on."

"That's right."

Miranda stared at him, raising an eyebrow, as they stood outside Winfred's house. "Why are you helping me with my article?"

"Because you need help."

She tilted her head as if she didn't appreciate that response.

"Let me take a few steps back here." Thaddeus realized how he sounded. "I just mean that whoever is behind everything that's happened isn't someone that you want to play with. You can go digging for answers all you want. You can write this article. But if you keep pushing, eventually you're going to run into danger again. I don't think you want to be alone when that happens. Do you?"

The blood seemed to drain from her face. "I have to admit I'd be powerless in the face of a weapon."

"That's what I thought. Besides, I'm curious about what's going on as well."

"Then I guess this makes sense. Us teaming up. Right?"

"Right. Besides, if something happened to you, that would ruin our friends' wedding."

Her lip curled slightly on the side. "We can't have that happen."

His lip curled also. "No, we can't." He nodded

back down the road. "Now how about if we get back before it gets dark?"

"That sounds like a great idea."

MIRANDA FELT the questions clashing inside her as she and Thaddeus walked back into Abigail's house. It appeared that neither Grant nor Abigail was there. Grant was probably still at the crime scene, and Abigail had said she'd be helping with the horses until late.

Maybe this would be the perfect time to tell Thaddeus what she needed to tell him.

Before Miranda could second-guess herself, she glanced up at him. "There's something that I want to show you."

"Okay . . ."

She nodded to her doorway, and he followed her there. Inside, she shut the door behind them, went to her dresser, and picked up the papers she'd taken from the motel. She'd laid them out earlier, trying to get them to dry. Much of the ink had blurred, but most of the text was still readable.

"I'd totally forgotten about these with everything else that's happened," she started. "But when we found those papers in that metal box, I shoved a few of them in my pocket. I didn't remember until earlier today that I had them. I'm not sure if they're significant or not."

Thaddeus took one of them and stared at her, confusion apparent with that knot between his eyes. "I'm not sure how these papers are going to help us."

"I don't think those papers are old. I know *the box* looked old, but the papers inside didn't. We assumed they were left from when the motel was still open. But what if this somehow ties in with the dead man instead?"

Thaddeus scanned the papers. "This looks like a list of names. I assumed it was probably a list of guests at the motel."

"But what if it's not? What if there's more to it?"

"It's definitely worth looking into—and showing Grant." He moved on to the next paper. "This looks like a map of something. But it's hand-drawn and hard to make out the words."

Miranda leaned closer. "I know. It could be a house. Maybe somebody was planning to break in somewhere?"

"I suppose it's a possibility." But Thaddeus sounded unconvinced. "It looks like an unusual layout for a house."

Just then, a sound came from her balcony.

Miranda and Thaddeus exchanged a look.

He'd heard it too.

It almost sounded like someone was trying to get inside.

CHAPTER TWENTY-ONE

"STAY HERE," Thaddeus told Miranda.

He reached for his gun as he strode toward the door. He had no idea what he expected to see on the other side.

But when he pulled the curtain back, he saw nothing.

For a moment, at least.

Then his gaze went to the box wrapped in brown paper that rested there.

"Is this yours?"

Miranda quickly shook her head. "No, I've never seen it before."

He craned his neck to see outside. But the darkness had already fallen, and it was nearly impossible to make anything out.

Still, if someone had just left this . . .

"Don't touch that," he muttered to Miranda. "I'll be back."

He tore down the hallway. The person who'd been on the balcony couldn't be far away. Thaddeus couldn't let this guy slip past. Not again.

He rushed down the steps, ran toward the road, and stopped. He glanced around, noting the other houses close to Abigail's.

The person who'd left that package could have run any direction and hidden behind multiple houses.

Carefully, he walked to the area where Miranda's balcony was located. Whoever left that box must have climbed up the live oak tree and grabbed onto the railing before breeching the side of the balcony.

He glanced in the sand and saw what appeared to be footprints.

Thaddeus tried to follow them, but they stopped near the dune.

Had the perpetrator escaped into the sea oats to conceal his prints?

Possibly.

As Thaddeus glanced around, he didn't see anyone.

Where had this guy gone?

It was clear he wasn't going to catch him now.

He needed to get back to Miranda and figure out what was in that box . . . he prayed she hadn't touched it while he was gone.

Because, at once, images of a bomb filled his mind.

What if there was something dangerous inside?

MIRANDA STARED AT THE PACKAGE. It was the size of a shoebox and wrapped in brown paper. From what she could see from where she stood, there was no writing on it.

But for someone to leave that on her balcony hadn't been easy. The person had gone through a lot of trouble to get it up there.

Clearly, whatever was inside was meant for Miranda.

This person would have had to know which room was hers and how to access the balcony.

A sickly feeling formed in her stomach.

What could be in it?

She took another step closer and stopped.

She'd promised Thaddeus she wouldn't touch it.

But, boy, did she want to.

What if it was more pictures? If someone wanted to further humiliate her?

Her heart pounded harder.

Part of her didn't want to find out.

Didn't want *Thaddeus* to find out.

As she heard a step behind her, she flinched and jolted back.

What if the person who'd left this had come inside while Thaddeus was gone? What if he wanted to confront her now?

She waited, unable to breathe, halfway expecting to see Brian's face.

Could he be behind this? Did he want to enact the ultimate revenge on her for breaking up with him?

The thought seemed ludicrous. But he was the one who'd gotten the receptionist at his gym fired because she hadn't checked him in in a timely manner. He'd also made life miserable for one of his coworkers until the man had finally quit.

He had a vindictive side to him.

But what if he wasn't behind this? Who would that leave then?

CHAPTER TWENTY-TWO

THADDEUS STEPPED into the room and saw Miranda pressed against the wall, a terrified look on her face. "Are you okay?"

Her shoulders slumped as she let out her breath. "It's only you."

Ordinarily, that greeting might set him back. But in this circumstance, he understood it.

"It's only me." He offered a weary grin.

She lowered her hand from over her heart. "Did you catch him?"

Thaddeus shook his head. "I wish I could say I did. But he had just enough of a head start to get away."

She frowned and let out another heavy breath. "Go figure."

He stared at her another moment, waiting for her to share whatever was on her mind.

When she didn't, Thaddeus finally asked, "You have an idea about who might have left this package, don't you?"

She stared at him a moment as if contemplating what to say. Finally, she rubbed her lips together and swallowed hard. "I can't stop wondering if Brian is behind this."

"Why would you think that? Because he said he'd do anything to win you back?"

"Yes. Or maybe it's one of those 'If I can't have you, no one can' type of things. Either way, I touched base with a couple of mutual friends I have in New York today. No one has seen him in two days."

His gaze met hers. "So, you think it's a possibility he followed you down here?"

Miranda shrugged. "I know it sounds crazy. But I suppose it's a possibility and that's why the thought won't leave my mind."

His jaw visibly tightened. "The paper that was left on the Jeep? Does that have something to do with this? Something to do with him?"

Her face went pale again. "No, I don't think so."

"Then what was it?" If they were going to be in this fight to stay alive together, then she needed to start sharing. He couldn't tiptoe around these questions any longer.

"Truthfully, it was just an old picture of me. Nothing really. Just meant to embarrass me."

"Do you happen to remember who took the picture of you? Where you were at the time? Do you know how someone could have gotten their hands on it?" Thaddeus assumed if it embarrassed her, she wouldn't have it posted on social media or shared it with anyone.

"It was from a while ago." She shook her head. "I really don't remember who took the picture. There's not even enough background showing for me to remember where I was at the time."

Thaddeus wondered what exactly about the picture embarrassed her. But he had a feeling he wouldn't get any more information out of Miranda now. It had clearly been hard for her to say as much as she had.

"What are we going to do about that box?" She stared at it on the patio.

There was only one thing that Thaddeus knew to do.

He needed to call Grant.

Maybe the department here had some type of bomb-sniffing dog. Until Thaddeus knew for sure that it was safe to open that package, he wasn't touching it.

Not given everything that had already happened.

AN HOUR LATER, the package had been cleared by Grant and his team.

No explosives were inside.

Miranda anxiously stood in the living room as she watched to see what the package actually held.

Dread filled her.

Would this be something dangerous? Humiliating?

It was anyone's guess at this point.

"Stay back, just in case," Grant said.

She inadvertently scooted closer to Thaddeus.

Even though the man had halfway broken her heart and she knew she should stay away, another part of her was still drawn to him. He still had that trustworthy vibe she'd first been attracted to. Even if his actions had proven that he wasn't trustworthy, her instincts told her she could trust him.

It didn't make sense.

Miranda remembered her vow not to think about the Thaddeus conundrum, and instead she watched as Grant pulled the brown paper from the box using gloved hands.

She held her breath as she waited to see what was inside.

A colorful card rested in layers of tissue paper there.

In the center of the design were the words, "Back off or boom! Don't make us tell you again."

Miranda let out a breath.

Someone had wanted to scare them. Had wanted them to think this was a bomb.

Disgust churned inside her.

"Someone wanted to make a point." Grant's voice hardened. "And they did."

"What now?" Miranda crossed her arms, not bothering to hide the tension pulsing through her body.

"I'll see if there are any prints on this. I doubt there are."

"And, until then, we just wait?" Miranda tried to keep the discouragement from her voice but failed. The tone was probably obvious to anyone listening.

"We'll sort through this as quickly as possible," Grant stated.

Thaddeus turned to Miranda. "Can we talk a moment?"

She nodded. "Of course."

He walked her to her room, out of earshot of everyone else. "Tomorrow, we investigate together, okay? You can't go out on your own. Please, promise me that."

"Why do you care what happens to me?" Miranda hadn't meant to ask the question, but it had slipped out anyway.

Frustration had taken hold. That, and a sense of defeat. She couldn't wrap her head around why this was happening. She also couldn't figure this man out no matter how hard she tried. He seemed like a walking contradiction.

"Why wouldn't I care?" He narrowed his eyes as he watched her expression.

She stared at him before shaking her head, her emotions surging and threatening to get the best of her. "You are one confusing male, Thaddeus Blackwell."

"And you are one confusing female, Miranda Stewart."

The two of them stared at each other another moment.

Miranda would never figure this man out.

If she knew what was best for her, she would stop trying.

CHAPTER TWENTY-THREE

THADDEUS, Grant, and Abigail sat at the table eating breakfast together the next morning. Grant had made ham and cheese omelets with extra sharp cheddar cheese melted over the top.

Miranda was still sleeping. Maybe yesterday had exhausted her.

"We're trying to get that permit to start digging." Grant cut into his omelet with his fork before stabbing a piece. "The unfortunate news is we probably won't know anything for sure until tomorrow."

"The day of your rehearsal dinner?" The timing on all this couldn't be worse.

"Unfortunately, yes." He frowned and glanced at his fiancée. "Remember, Abigail and I have to go to the courthouse this morning to pick up our marriage license. Are you and Miranda going to be okay here alone?"

"We should be fine."

"What do you think you two will do today?" Abigail stared at him, blinking a little too sweetly.

"I'm sure we'll find something to occupy ourselves. Maybe we'll drive around and look at the wild horses." Thaddeus took another long sip of coffee, not wanting to expound on the subject.

"Feel free to use my truck as much as you need it," Grant offered. "I had Dash stop by so we could fix those wires. You know where the keys are."

"I hope that you have a great time together," Abigail said.

Thaddeus sent her a look, knowing exactly what she was getting at. Abigail was still rooting for the two of them to get together. That was probably why she'd requested he and Miranda come into town so early.

But becoming involved with Miranda wasn't going to happen. Not in a romantic sense, at least. He couldn't let himself be drawn in again.

Grant and Abigail left several minutes later, and no sooner had the front door shut did Miranda come out freshly showered wearing jeans and a T-shirt.

Her hair was pulled back in a casual ponytail, and her face was absent of any makeup.

She smiled shyly at him as she stepped closer.

Shyly? That didn't fit the woman he knew.

Then again, Thaddeus just couldn't figure her out.

"Good morning," she started. "I waited until Grant and Abigail left to come out because I wasn't sure if I could conceal what we were doing. I didn't want to be put through all the questions."

Thaddeus held back a smile. "Probably a good idea then."

She glanced at her watch. "We have a lot to get done while they're gone. Are you ready to go?"

"You don't want to eat first?" He nodded at the omelet Grant had made for her, and the sides of bacon and muffins left on the table.

She plucked a muffin from the table and held it up. "This will be good. And coffee. Just let me grab a cup to go."

Thaddeus watched her as she hurried into the kitchen. As he did, he realized this was going to be a very interesting day.

Definitely more than he bargained for when he'd bought his plane ticket to come here.

AS THADDEUS PULLED up in front of Winfred's house, Miranda stared at it for a moment.

Today, an old truck was parked beneath the stilted structure.

Hopefully, that meant the man was home.

"I'll take the lead," Thaddeus told Miranda as they climbed from the truck and began walking toward the house.

She didn't argue. Instead, Miranda stayed by Thaddeus' side as he knocked at Winfred's door.

The sound of a TV permeated the walls. The morning news blared, an anchor doing a rundown of the headlines, including a football update, a report on a string of bank robberies down south, and the potential for bad weather later on.

However, no one answered the door.

Miranda stepped back and looked at Thaddeus. "He could be in the shower."

Thaddeus narrowed his gaze, clearly not agreeing that was the case. Instead, he knocked again, harder this time.

They waited again, but there was still no answer.

Thaddeus paced from the door to the edge of the deck, and he peered over.

The next instant, he yelled, "Hey!" Then he took off running.

Miranda glanced around the edge of the house and spotted a man darting across the street.

Winfred must have left out the back door.

She followed behind Thaddeus, knowing she wouldn't be able to keep up. She'd never been a fast runner.

Thaddeus on the other hand was surprisingly agile in his cowboy boots.

Within moments, he tackled the man to the sand, and Winfred hit the ground with an umph.

Miranda caught up with them just in time to hear Winfred complain, "What do you think you're doing? Get off me."

Thaddeus stood and hauled the man to his feet. "You have some explaining to do."

CHAPTER TWENTY-FOUR

THADDEUS STARED at the man standing in front of him. Winfred was younger than he'd thought. His bald head had made him seem older from a distance. Up close he looked no older than his late thirties, at the most.

But the fear in the man's eyes was clear.

"I didn't do anything wrong." Winfred's words were spoken with both a lisp and a thick country accent, a mix that was difficult to understand.

"Then why were you running?" Thaddeus demanded. "Usually only guilty people run."

"I ran because you looked aggressive. I heard you were a fed."

"I am a fed, but I'm not trying to be aggressive,"

Thaddeus muttered. "I just need to ask you some questions."

His eyes remained wide, and he shifted from one foot to the other as if contemplating running again. "About what?"

"Knobs Hill."

Winfred's shoulders seemed to stiffen. "What do you want to know about that place?"

Thaddeus watched him carefully to make sure he wasn't going to take off again. The man's actions made him seem dishonorable, like he was a part of whatever was going on there.

Miranda stood close, listening to the conversation.

"We heard you've been digging there," Thaddeus began. "We want to know why."

"Digging?" He jerked his lip up, revealing several missing teeth. "Who told you that?"

"It doesn't matter. Some strange things have been going on there lately, and your name came up."

"I wasn't doing anything wrong," Winfred said. "I was just looking for something."

"The old motel maybe?" Thaddeus took a step closer.

"Why does the FBI care?"

"The FBI doesn't care, but I do. I almost got

killed because of that old motel. Now I need answers."

The man's eyes widened as if realization dawned. "That old motel has always been trouble. Nobody around here wanted it built to begin with. Why would I want to find it?"

"That's what we would like to know." Thaddeus resisted the urge to roll his eyes. Why did this guy have to draw this out so long?

Winfred raised his hands as if sensing Thaddeus' irritation. "Look, the only reason I was out there digging was because about five years ago I buried a time capsule. Now I want it back."

Thaddeus stared at him, not hiding the fact that he thought this guy's story seemed unlikely.

"What? It's true." Winfred's lisp deepened. "I don't care how it sounds. I just . . . I can't find it, okay?"

"Why do you want this time capsule so badly?" Miranda asked.

"My brother's watch is in it. He passed away about two months ago. So now I'd like to have that watch back. It's sentimental."

Thaddeus mentally shook his head. This guy looked anything but sentimental.

"And you have no idea where you buried it on the hill?" Miranda continued.

"As you've probably heard, that sand dune keeps shifting. So, there's no guarantee where it is now. I know what you're thinking. That Knobs Hill was a horrible place to bury something like that. But, at the time, I was half drunk, so it made sense to me."

Thaddeus stared at him another moment. He believed at least part of Winfred's story—the getting drunk part of it.

Hardening his gaze, Thaddeus silently dared the man to lie. "Is there anything else that you can tell me about that place?"

Winfred shrugged. "I've been there several times recently trying to find that dang time capsule. I have seen some movement out there at night. But I didn't pay any attention to it."

"What kind of movement?" Miranda stepped closer, her eyes narrowed as she processed what he'd told them.

"I just said I didn't pay any attention."

Thaddeus took a step closer to the man.

"Okay. Okay." Winfred held up his hands. "Some people were down where the dune meets Wash Woods. I'm not used to seeing people out there. Just horses. That's all I can tell you. I couldn't see what they were doing or anything."

"Could you identify any of them if you saw them again?" Thaddeus asked.

Winfred ran a hand over his head. "Nope. Didn't see them close enough."

Thaddeus stared at him another moment before realizing he'd asked everything that he had to ask.

Yet he and Miranda still were no closer to finding the answers they were searching for.

MIRANDA AND THADDEUS climbed back into the truck and sat for a moment in silence. Miranda's thoughts raced through what had just happened.

"Not as fruitful as we would have hoped, right?" Miranda started.

Thaddeus lifted his cowboy hat long enough to run a hand through his hair and let out a sigh. "No, not exactly. Whatever is going on here, I don't like it."

"When Winfred said something about you being a fed, that reminded me I meant to ask you something. Did I hear you telling Grant that you took a leave of absence from the FBI?" She turned toward him as a shadow fell over Thaddeus' gaze.

"I did." His voice tightened.

"Why? You really seemed to love working for the FBI. You told me on our date that it was all you'd ever wanted to do." She clamped down after she asked the question. It had been her suggestion yesterday to forget that date ever happened. Now here she was talking about it. "Never mind. I shouldn't have asked."

"No, it's okay." He shrugged. "I just started back a few weeks ago, so I'm on the job again. For a little while, at least."

Miranda wondered what had happened. It had to be big if he'd taken significant time off. Thaddeus didn't seem like the type to take extended breaks.

Except when it came to her. She frowned at the thought.

"Something must have happened. I'm guessing?"

"It's . . . it's a long story," Thaddeus finally offered.

Clearly, he didn't want to talk about it.

Miranda cleared her throat instead, not wanting to be the one who didn't get the hint.

She let out a sigh as she changed the subject. "So, what should we do now?"

He leaned back in his seat, almost as if relieved

for the shift in conversation. "What about that man that Hillsdale mentioned? Jared? The man who used to live at the Sand Spur and who was upset when the motel closed. Maybe we could go pay him a visit."

"It's worth a shot at this point. But we'll need to find his address first."

"I bet Emmy knows it. Let me give her a call."

"I can call her," Miranda offered.

"You have her number?"

"We exchanged numbers the other day, just in case we needed to do anything else for Abigail."

A few minutes later, Miranda had the information they needed, and they took off down the road.

As they did, Miranda glanced at her phone and saw she had a message from one of Brian's friends. She'd texted him yesterday and said she was trying to get up with Brian but couldn't reach him and was worried.

Brian's been hiking in Arizona this week. He should be back in a few days. Try him again then.

She frowned. What sense did that make? Because if Brian was in Arizona, that meant he wasn't the one she'd seen watching her or who'd left that picture on the Jeep. So who did those things? Who left the box on her balcony, for that matter?

"Everything okay?" Thaddeus cast a quick glance at her.

She quickly lowered her phone. "I guess. Except . . . Brian's friend said he's in Arizona right now."

"How do you know his friend isn't lying?"

Miranda shrugged. "I suppose he could be covering for him. He doesn't seem like the type to lie but . . ."

"Anyone is capable of lying if the stakes are high enough," Thaddeus said.

The way he said the words made her think there was more to them than just this conversation.

Whatever had happened to him back in Austin must have been devastating.

But the last thing Miranda wanted was to warm her heart to him again.

Because her heart was already in a fragile state right now, and she didn't think she could handle having it hurt anymore.

CHAPTER TWENTY-FIVE

FOR A MOMENT, Thaddeus felt like he was back in Austin tracking down leads for a case.

So much of what he did wasn't glamorous like some people thought. His work involved filling out paperwork, talking to people, making phone calls, and filling out more paperwork. The cycle could be monotonous.

Sometimes those people gave him honest answers and sometimes they didn't. Sometimes their responses directed him toward the truth, and other times those responses were purposefully misleading.

He hoped this talk with Jared might go better than his talk with Winfred. He wanted a resolution to this, sooner rather than later. The box placed on

Miranda's balcony had left him uneasy, to say the least.

He didn't like where this whole situation was going.

He and Miranda found Jared on the dock behind the man's waterfront house. Jared was in his fifties with faded blond hair and leathery skin with too many wrinkles to count. He wore dirty clothes and shoes with holes at the toes. Several beer cans littered the dock around him.

"What can I help you with?" Jared didn't bother to even turn his head as he continued fishing.

"Hoping to ask you a few questions about the old Sand Spur Motel," Thaddeus started.

"What about it?"

"We understand that you used to live there," Thaddeus said. "Is that correct?"

"I did. Renting a room was cheaper than trying to buy property on the island . . . and I didn't have to clean up after myself."

"You were upset when it was about to be closed," Miranda said. "Is that also correct?"

"Of course, I was upset. I had to find a new place to live. I didn't understand why the county wasn't doing more to prevent the sand dune from destroying the place."

"You do realize that would have cost millions of dollars." Thaddeus wasn't experienced with how things worked in this area. But he could only imagine how expensive that proposition might have been.

"They spend money on what they want. It's all about who you know."

Thaddeus couldn't deny the truth in his words. That was spot on across the board, not just here in Cape Corral.

"Why are you coming around asking about that old place?" He paused from fishing and glanced back as he asked the question.

"There's been some activity there lately, and we're trying to figure out what's going on," Thaddeus said. "Have you heard anything about it?"

"People wouldn't talk to me about anything happening over there."

"But have you seen anything?"

Jared set his fishing pole in a rod holder and crossed his arms as he turned toward them. "They closed the motel a good while before the storm came through that finished burying the place. During that time, there were some activities going on there. It was the perfect location. Secluded. No one ever went back there. So, yeah, I know some drug deals happened. But after it was buried, nobody could get to it."

"So how would somebody get inside it now?" Miranda slid on her sunglasses, probably to ward off the glare from the water. "You used to live there. Is there any way you can think of?"

He rubbed his chin. "I can't say that I know of anything."

"What about underground? Some kind of tunnel or pipes maybe?"

"Every place on this island has its own septic system, so there are no pipes or drains or anything like that connecting any buildings—not ones big enough to fit through, at least. The island's below the sea level, so they can't do that around here. And building a tunnel in sand? I'd like to see someone try."

"That's what I assumed." But Thaddeus had wanted to ask, just in case.

It looked like this interview was also getting them nowhere. He glanced at Miranda, and she shrugged as if she also had no more questions.

Thaddeus took a step away. "Thank you for your time."

"Wait a second. There is one thing that I can tell you."

Thaddeus paused and turned back toward the man. "What's that?"

Jared remained where he was, still staring at them, even though something tugged on his fishing line. "Sometimes I go fishing out that way and I'll stay until after the sun has set. Several times I've seen boats running up to that area at night and docking by Wash Woods. My guess is the guys onboard are cutting through the woods and doing something they don't want to be seen doing."

Thaddeus stored that information. "How many times have you seen this happen?"

"Four or five."

"Did you actually see anyone enter the woods after getting off the boat?" Miranda clarified.

"No, but anything you do that late at night usually isn't above par, if you know what I mean. Take it from me. I would know. But I'm reformed now, and I don't like trouble."

Thaddeus knew *exactly* what the man meant.

But how was he going to catch these guys red-handed when they came back next time?

MIRANDA AND THADDEUS headed back to Abigail's. They'd already discussed their conversation with Jared. Now, they'd decided to grab a bite to eat and spell out everything they knew in order to form a plan of action.

She hoped they could make some headway.

"I'm going to have to get some barbecue sometime," Thaddeus muttered as he peered into the fridge. "Ever since I smelled Hillsdale smoking that pork outside his house, I've been longing for a good old Texas cookout."

"That barbecue we had in Austin was insanely good." Miranda joined him in the kitchen.

"I know, right?" He glanced back at her. "That place is the best. I probably go once a week."

Did he take a different woman each time? Was he that kind of guy?

She frowned. She didn't think so. Maybe she just had to come to terms with the fact that she wasn't his type, despite the chemistry they shared.

But, before they could make any sandwiches, a shadow filled one of the front windows.

The next instant, the window shattered as bullets pierced the air.

Miranda gasped and ducked behind the kitchen doorway as another bullet flew through the house and embedded itself into the wall on the opposite side.

She glanced at Thaddeus who'd moved behind the other side of the door frame. "What's happening right now?"

He withdrew his gun and held it in front of him. "This guy's getting bolder, that's what's happening."

How many times could they avoid death before it found them? Whoever was after them was relentless. "We're going to die, aren't we?" Her voice cracked with fear.

Thaddeus' gaze met hers and held. "Stay positive. I *am* an FBI agent."

Miranda tried to keep that fact in mind. This man was a trained fed. He wasn't like Brian, who'd worked in an office all day, drank pour-over coffees, and ate unpronounceable foods, all while manscaping himself so he could take Instagram-worthy pictures.

Thaddeus could hold his own in a fight. She'd seen it firsthand when he'd tackled Winfred to the ground. But then again, Winfred hadn't had a gun and bullets hadn't been flying.

As another bullet pierced the air, Thaddeus turned. He aimed his gun and fired several shots.

The sound of the discharge made her ears ring.

Every blast made her flinch. The acidic scent of smoke made her sick to her stomach.

Silence stretched for a moment.

Had the shooter been hit?

Or was the gunman getting closer? Planning something new?

Miranda had no idea. She only knew that fear slithered up her spine, held her immobile.

As another bullet split the door frame beside her, she swallowed back a scream.

Thaddeus fired back.

Whoever was trying to kill them wasn't giving up. It was becoming more and more difficult to stay positive.

Miranda had simply come to town to help with Abigail's wedding. How had her trip turned into such chaos?

Enduring a gunfight?

This just seemed surreal.

As she heard the front door burst open and heavy footsteps pound inside, she knew their trouble was far from over.

Whoever was after them was closing in.

She swallowed back a scream.

Part of her wanted to close her eyes and pretend

this wasn't happening, because the possibilities of what could happen next were too terrifying.

Just as the thought crossed her mind, she heard another blast.

Then something sharp cut into her arm.

CHAPTER TWENTY-SIX

THADDEUS SAW the blood flood Miranda's shirtsleeve.

She'd been hit!

He wanted nothing more than to cross the space and reach her.

But he couldn't.

Not while this guy was firing.

"Grab that dish towel and press it on your wound," he instructed.

Her skin looked pale, but she did as he said.

It appeared to be only a surface wound. He prayed that was the case.

"Give it back to me, and maybe I'll let you live," a man's deep voice sounded as the gunfire halted for a moment.

Give what back? What was the guy even talking about?

Thaddeus didn't wait to find out. He leaned out of the doorway and pulled his trigger again.

But his gun just clicked.

Thaddeus was out of bullets. He didn't have any more with him right now. He hadn't even brought that many on this trip, considering he was coming to a wedding. He'd never expected to find all this trouble.

"Thaddeus?" Miranda's voice trembled as she stared at him from the other side of the doorway.

"Just stay where you are," he murmured.

But as he heard another footstep coming his way, he knew they were in trouble. The man had a gun and Thaddeus was out of bullets. The odds of them coming out of this alive were growing slimmer with each passing moment.

But he'd do whatever was in his power to protect Miranda.

Just then, sirens sounded outside.

The footsteps stopped.

Dash must be here. Someone must have heard gunfire and called the police.

Footsteps began running in the opposite direction.

Thaddeus couldn't let this guy get away. "Stay here," he whispered to Miranda.

Then he took off after the gunman.

The man was already outside. Thaddeus sprinted through the foyer and out the door. He leaped over the balcony and onto the sand before taking off.

Thaddeus spotted Dash dart from his truck and chase the man on foot. The shooter, dressed all in black, maneuvered under a nearby house, having a decent head start on Dash.

Thaddeus wanted to continue chasing him also.

But he needed to help Miranda.

He hurried back inside and paused in front of her as she cowered near the wall. Blood stained the dish towel she held against her bicep. "Let me see your arm."

She didn't move, a far-off look in her eyes.

Was she reliving the robbery she'd told him about? The one where the man had held a gun to her head?

He could only imagine the trauma going on inside her mind right now.

"It's okay. You're safe now."

Miranda snapped her gaze to his as if realizing where she was and what was happening. "Where did he go?" Her voice trembled as she asked the question.

He placed a hand on her arm, trying to ground her. "Dash is chasing him."

"You came back for me?" An unreadable emotion rushed across her face.

"You were shot. Of course I came back."

"I'm fine. It's just a flesh wound. Nothing too serious."

He wasn't sure about that.

This whole situation was spinning out of control, and it didn't seem to be slowing down anytime soon.

He led her to a kitchen chair and sat her down, instructing her to take some deep breaths.

She was safe for now. But how was he going to keep her that way?

He was no longer sure that he could.

His throat tightened at the thought.

But he would die trying, he vowed.

Because this was personal now.

WHEN MIRANDA SAW the protectiveness in Thaddeus' eyes, she felt her heart lodge in her throat.

Why did he have to look at her like that? His

concerned gaze made her want to turn back time. Made her want to give this guy a chance again.

But doing so could be fatal—for her heart, at least. Especially since it had ended in rejection before.

As a shadow filled the doorway, she sucked in a breath and braced herself for more danger. Thaddeus turned also, his shoulders broadening as if he were becoming a human shield.

Had the gunman somehow circled back around and come back?

She could hardly breathe.

But instead of a man with a gun, a familiar face stared at them.

Where had Miranda seen the guy with shaggy blond hair and a crooked nose before?

The man raised his hands. "I'm just here to clean the hot tub."

Miranda released her breath. That was right. The pool guy. Stephen.

"You just got here?" Thaddeus stood.

"Yeah."

"Did you see anything when you were outside? Somebody running from the house?"

Stephen shrugged. "When I pulled down the road, I saw Officer Fulton running toward something in the distance. But that's all I saw. Why? What's going on?"

"Somebody was just shooting at us," Thaddeus said.

Stephen stood awkwardly in the doorway, his gaze shifting to Miranda and his eyes narrowing when he glanced at her arm. "You got shot?"

"I'm fine." She pressed her hand over the wound. "It's just a scratch."

"Seems nowhere is safe these days." He paused. "Okay then. So, uh . . . should I go clean the hot tub?"

"I thought you did that yesterday," Miranda muttered, her thoughts racing. Was this man's appearance here right now suspicious?

Stephen shrugged. "I came, but I didn't have one of the chemicals I needed. I told Abigail I'd come back today after I picked up some more."

Thaddeus waved a hand, motioning that this wasn't a big deal. "Why don't you hold off on that until tomorrow? Now's not a good time."

"I can see that." He glanced at the bullet holes in the walls. "This used to be such a peaceful place."

"Have you lived here for a long time?" Thaddeus narrowed his gaze as if he might interrogate the man.

"Long enough to know this isn't normal. I moved

here when I was eighteen so I could get away from the hustle of the American dream, if you know what I mean. My American dream didn't require working twelve-hour days five or six days a week."

Miranda could understand that. Her job was demanding—as evidenced by the dozens of emails her editor had sent Miranda while she was here officially on vacation. Her job wasn't just a job. It was a lifestyle.

Was that what she really wanted?

"You work a lot of the homes here on the island?" Thaddeus asked Stephen.

"That's right." Stephen shifted as if bracing himself for more questions.

"You notice anything strange or out of the ordinary?"

Stephen stared off in the distance a moment before sighing. "Not really. I mean, you get all types of interesting people on the island. Families on vacation, fishermen, people just wanting to get away and work remotely for a while. It's not the vacationers who give me pause."

"What do you mean?"

He stepped closer. "Between you and me . . . I've seen some people hanging out down in Wash Woods. The house my friend and I are renting isn't too far from there. They always seem to be there at night, like they're sneaking around. I heard a rumor that they were shooting at something the other day. If you ask me, that place is the heart of all this trouble."

"That's very interesting," Thaddeus said.

"I thought so too." Stephen shrugged. "Anyway, I'll come back tomorrow. Sorry to bother you."

As Stephen nodded and disappeared, Miranda let out another breath.

Why did danger keep coming at them from every angle?

CHAPTER TWENTY-SEVEN

DASH APPEARED A FEW MINUTES LATER. He got their statements, took photos of the bullet holes, and collected shell casings.

While a paramedic treated Miranda inside, Thaddeus accompanied Dash outside.

"Do you have any idea what's going on here?" Dash looked up at Thaddeus as he took an impression of a footprint in the sand. "Grant told me a few things, but why did this guy come to Abigail's house?"

"My guess is that Miranda and I either have something this guy wants, or he wants to silence us because he thinks we know something."

"Either way, we're going to find that body in the motel." Dash's voice showed his determination.

"Not if they've moved it." Thaddeus didn't like the grim tone to his voice, but he knew his words were true.

Dash paused, waiting for the impression to dry, and glanced at Thaddeus. "How would this guy get down there to do that?"

"There has to be another way they're getting in."

Dash narrowed his eyes. "Maybe. But we've searched the area around Knobs Hill. We didn't see anything."

"There are a lot of things about this case that aren't making sense. We're missing some key pieces of this puzzle that we need in order to find any of these answers."

"I'd say so." Dash glanced at a bullet hole in the side of the house and sighed. "I'm going to need to call Abigail and let her know what happened. I hate to do it, especially so close to the wedding."

Thaddeus frowned also. "I wish we could clean this up before she comes home, but Grant will want to see this himself."

Dash let out another long breath. "Yes, he will. I'll call and let them know what happened. You and Miranda just take care of yourselves for now."

Thaddeus thought about Miranda and felt a new

heaviness on his chest. Exactly what had they gotten themselves into?

CHAPTER TWENTY-EIGHT

"ARE you sure you want to go out to Wash Woods?" Thaddeus locked gazes with Miranda as they stood in the foyer of Abigail's place.

Four hours had passed since the gunman invaded this home. Miranda's arm now had butterfly bandages where the bullet had grazed her skin. Grant and Abigail were on their way back but hadn't arrived yet. Just as Thaddeus suspected, Grant had wanted them to leave the scene as it was. He wanted to see it for himself.

"I don't think we have much choice at this point." Miranda shrugged, looking neither excited nor fearful. "Time is running out. The wedding is coming up. You and I both have to leave soon after. My career possibly depends on this. Maybe yours does too."

Thaddeus stared at her face another moment, wanting to deny her words. But he couldn't. There was a lot riding on this, and he couldn't see himself going back to Texas after this without any answers.

"You have to promise me that you're going to be careful." He stepped closer and lowered his voice.

She swallowed hard before nodding. "I will be. I won't be brash or make any sudden moves. I'll let you call the shots . . . for the most part."

Thaddeus raised an eyebrow. "For the most part?"

"I mean, I don't want to lock myself into that promise if push comes to shove. If you're dying, I'm not going to wait for you to give me the word to step in and help." Her eyes appeared wide with sincerity.

Miranda may have been overthinking this just a bit.

Instead of arguing, he simply nodded and took her arm. "Then let's go."

As they stepped out to the truck, Thaddeus hoped he didn't regret doing this. There was no telling what would happen out in Wash Woods tonight.

It could be nothing. That's the way Jared made it sound.

But the lead was at least worth looking into to see if anything was going on. Maybe they could find evidence of *something* in the woods.

The ride to Wash Woods was mostly quiet. Thaddeus parked the truck in a small public lot. They'd have to go the rest of the way on foot.

He wasn't sure what the conditions would be like, but he remembered the quicksand Grant had told him about. The wild boars. The snakes.

Before getting out of the truck, Thaddeus turned toward her. "Let's walk through the woods and see what we can find. Make sure you bring your backpack with you, just in case."

"I will. As the saying goes, here goes nothing."

Thaddeus gripped his backpack as they started into the forest. The woods were thick with slender trees crowding close together and low branches that spindled like webs. Seedlings grew at their feet, and the ground was soft with sand and water.

He wanted to make it to the area Jared mentioned seeing those boats dock. Then, from there, they'd walk to Knobs Hill.

"Are you an outside girl?" he asked Miranda, curious to see what she'd say.

"I used to love being outside when I was a girl," she started. "My mom and I had a small house, but it was on an acre of land that used to be my grandmother's. I loved exploring the woods behind it and skipping rocks in the creek."

He smiled. "Sounds nice."

"I made a fort, and I would take my books and read out there while my mom worked. She had to have two jobs, so I was on my own a lot. It's one reason why I vowed to go to college and get a job that could support me."

"That's great that you were able to do that."

"I worked hard on my grades and ended up getting scholarships that basically paid for my entire education."

Impressive. "What did you do after college?"

"I worked for a couple of local magazines in Ohio—that's where I grew up. But New York had always been my goal. It was the mecca of publishing in my mind. I got a job there, but it was for an engineering magazine. I hated it. I got my current job . . . a couple of weeks after I went to Austin, actually."

Interesting. He wondered if there was some correlation between that timeline and the change he'd seen in her.

It didn't really matter.

So why did he have to keep reminding himself of that fact?

MIRANDA DIDN'T WANT to admit it, but she enjoyed talking to Thaddeus as they walked.

He seemed like an all-around good person.

Maybe she should simply ask him why he'd never called. Why was it so hard for her to do that? Was it easier to live with the unknowns than it was to face the truth?

Maybe the truth was that she feared facing his rejection again. Or his honest assessment of what was wrong with her. Or the fact that he might admit Miranda didn't live up to his expectations.

She had heard all those things before.

Each time, the criticism seemed to brew something deep inside her.

Miranda told herself that her confidence shouldn't come from things like other people's opinions or a number on a scale or how she compared to other more beautiful women around her.

Those insecurities were her flesh-and-blood struggles. They always had been. It didn't matter how she'd transformed herself on the outside . . . those ghosts from her past still haunted her.

Sometimes, she missed those days when image wasn't important to her. She missed not caring about trends or how fashionable she looked.

But maybe that would change. Maybe all she needed was her big break right now.

With any luck, this excursion would do the trick. She could write that article, find another job, and stop pretending to be someone she wasn't.

"You're being quiet back there." Thaddeus pushed another thick section of tree branches out of the way.

A million things yet nothing, Miranda thought to herself. She wasn't sure she wanted to share her thoughts with Thaddeus. Even if she did, walking through the woods might not be the ideal place to do so.

She needed to get this man out of her head. Yet how could she?

If she let down her guard for just a moment, she would be swept away by him again. He just had that effect on her for some reason. She'd never experienced anything like it before.

"What's on your mind?" he asked.

"I'm just watching where I'm going," Miranda finally said. "And looking for snakes."

"Probably a good idea."

Finally, the horizon cleared in the distance. As they stepped through the brush, they reached a sandy area that stretched out into the calm waters of the Currituck Sound. In the distance, two horses stood in shallow water, forming a beautiful picture.

Miranda continued to stare at the scene. This whole island was just so stunning. She could see why people liked living here in Cape Corral.

In some ways, this place was like stepping back in time. Miranda had to wonder if there were some on the island who might wish the bridge was never fixed. Its absence kept the community isolated. In some ways, it kept the area more protected.

"How would you like that view every morning?" Thaddeus followed her gaze.

"I wouldn't complain, that's for sure. How about you?"

"I thought looking across the Texas plains was amazing. And it is. But there's something about this that's also breathtaking."

They stood silently beside each other a moment, catching their breath and regrouping their thoughts.

Thaddeus cleared his throat and turned back to her. "All right, so we're going to assume that these guys are pulling up their boat somewhere in this general vicinity. I'm wondering if they're docking then walking through the woods to the motel at Knobs Hill."

"Which is buried." Miranda tried to picture it.

"Exactly. I know it's a longshot that we'll find anything. But unless we look, we won't know for sure."

"Then let's keep going." Miranda pulled her flannel shirt closer and nodded toward the woods again.

She really hoped this entire trek wasn't for nothing.

CHAPTER TWENTY-NINE

THE BEST THADDEUS COULD TELL, they were halfway between the Currituck Sound and Knobs Hill. There was no direct path, so they had to forge their own.

The brush was thick. At times, it was wet. Sometimes, even though it was October, it was buggy.

Overall, Miranda was holding up surprisingly well. She hadn't complained or stumbled or freaked out.

Maybe she wasn't as much of a city slicker as he thought.

A noise in the distance caught his ear, and he paused. He raised his hand, motioning for Miranda to stop also and then placed a finger over his lips.

What was that he'd heard?

Miranda paused beside him, her eyes wide as she glanced around.

There it was again. The sound.

Voices.

They were getting louder, coming this way.

Thaddeus and Miranda ducked farther into the brush to avoid being seen.

He prayed Miranda could stay quiet enough for them to remain in hiding.

In the distance, he spotted two figures clad in black walking in the brush. From a distance, Thaddeus couldn't make out any of their details or understand any of their words.

Were these the guys who were behind all this?

There hadn't been a boat at the dock, so there was no reason for Thaddeus to think these guys would be here right now.

Unless they were only using those boats for a specific purpose—like to be more secretive and hide their illegal actions. Otherwise, they could have parked a vehicle somewhere and walked from there.

"What are we going to do?" Miranda whispered as she crouched out of sight.

Thaddeus placed his finger over his mouth again. "We don't want to let them know we're here. I need to get closer, but I want you to stay here."

She frowned but nodded. "Understood."

Just as she said the words, she gasped.

Thaddeus glanced down in time to see a horsefly buzz away—but only after leaving a welt on her skin. That had to hurt.

His gaze shot to the men.

The men froze and glanced their way.

They must have heard Miranda's gasp.

Thaddeus braced himself for whatever might happen.

The next instant, a bullet sliced the air.

MIRANDA DUCKED as she heard the gun blast again.

"We've got to run," Thaddeus rushed.

"What?" Fear pulsed through her. "Can't you just shoot back?"

"I only want to use the gun if absolutely necessary. Just trust me." Thaddeus grabbed her hand and began pulling her through the woods.

Miranda hardly knew what was happening. Only that branches slapped her. Roots tried to trip her. Thaddeus' hand gripped hers so hard her fingers hurt.

None of that mattered.

The only thing that mattered was getting away from the gunmen.

At the thought, another bullet cut through the air.

Footsteps pounded behind them.

These men were chasing them.

The next instant, Thaddeus tugged her to the ground.

Plants surrounded them. Poked them. Entrapped them.

Hid them.

"If we stay low, they won't see us here," he whispered, his body partially covering hers. He reached for his holster and pulled out his gun, gripping it as if preparing to use it.

Could they hide? Was Thaddeus right? Miranda had no reason to think he wasn't.

Granted, she had trust issues. Lots of trust issues. Abandonment issues.

But she was going to do her best to rely on Thaddeus right now.

She didn't have much choice.

CHAPTER THIRTY

THADDEUS BRACED himself for whatever might happen next. He knew if he pulled the trigger that a gunfight could occur—one that could end up deadly. That wasn't what he wanted.

But he would use his weapon if necessary.

The footsteps were close.

Really close.

Then the voices came. Two of them.

"Where'd they go? They can't just disappear."

"They're around here somewhere."

"I think they turned the other direction. That one guy . . . he's an FBI agent. I heard some people in town talking about him."

Thaddeus listened to the men talk. Why did one of them sound familiar?

He couldn't place where he'd heard that voice before, and face buffs covered the men's faces, concealing their identity.

Miranda let out a whimper beneath him as if she was having trouble holding her fear in.

He smoothed her hair back, trying to reassure her.

They could still get out of this alive. They just needed to be quiet.

"Should we go the other direction?" one man asked.

"I guess so. I don't see them around here anywhere. Better yet, let's go before they see us again."

"You sure?"

"I'm as sure about this as I'm sure about the fact we're going to be rich."

The men chuckled.

Thaddeus waited, making sure this wasn't a trap.

Footsteps faded, as did the rustling in the brush.

Still, Thaddeus waited, just to be on the safe side.

He glanced at Miranda's wide, terrified eyes, and he tried to reassure her with his gaze.

They were so close to walking away from this.

He prayed nothing happened to ruin it now.

MIRANDA TRIED to catch her breath as anxiety squeezed her lungs. She waited several minutes after the voices faded to ask, "Did we lose them?"

"I think so," Thaddeus murmured in her ear as he eased off her.

She swatted a fly from her face, knowing this was a horrible time to get the creepy-crawlies. But between the soggy ground beneath her, the grass tickling her skin, and the flies, she felt like she could crawl out of her skin.

"Do you think those were the guys we were looking for?" she whispered.

"That's my best guess."

"Maybe we can still go after them, see if we can get a better look at who they are."

"It's too risky, especially since I don't have any backup out here."

Miranda bit back her disappointment, even though she understood what he was saying.

Instead, she observed the dense brush around her. The foliage made her feel like she was lost in the middle of the jungle somewhere instead of on a North Carolina island. Not that there were palm trees or jungle-like plants around her. But everything was just so green and thick.

After several more minutes, Thaddeus finally stood and helped her up.

"We need to keep moving," he muttered.

She didn't argue. She was ready to get out of this place.

She swatted at her face, still feeling insects bombing her.

Thaddeus took her hand and led her in the opposite direction of where the men had headed. They remained close to the edge of the woods, near where the trees met a long, winding stretch of Knobs Hill.

She assumed this area would be flat, but a surprising number of hills and ravines made the woods seem mountainous. As they climbed down into one of those gulches, her foot hit a root.

She stumbled forward, reaching out her hand to brace herself.

Her fingers touched something . . . solid.

"Thaddeus . . ." she muttered as she stared at a thick cluster of trees and vines.

"What is it?" Thaddeus turned back toward her.

"I'm not sure." Miranda took another step

forward, trying to figure out what she was touching that didn't quite feel normal.

She moved several vines away from the wall of trees in front of her.

Her eyes widened at what she saw there.

A tunnel protruded into the sand. Plywood and scaffolding held up the walls.

"I guess you can build a tunnel in the sand after all," Miranda muttered. "I've never seen anything like it."

The dark corridor stared back at them, just daring them to step inside.

CHAPTER THIRTY-ONE

"IS this what I think it is?" Thaddeus mumbled as he stared at the tunnel beneath the dune. Trees grew on top of it, placing it farther away from the area where Grant and his guys had searched.

"It has to be." Fascination captured the wispy tones of Miranda's voice. "This is how these guys are getting in and out of the motel. They built a tunnel to reach it."

He took a step forward and peered at the makeshift walls. "This can't be safe."

"It's been reenforced with scaffolding." Miranda leaned closer as she studied it. "What do you say? Should we check it out?"

Thaddeus didn't even have to think about his

answer. "No. Definitely no. This whole thing could collapse."

Her gaze locked onto his. "We can't just walk away now."

"Sure, we can. We can walk away from here and call Grant to let him know what we found." Going inside would be a bad, bad idea. He needed to make that clear.

"What if those guys come back? What if they got spooked and come back to hide clues that we need to find?"

"We? You mean, that *law enforcement* needs to find." Did she even hear herself?

Miranda shrugged, clearly unaffected by his words. "Same smell."

Thaddeus stepped closer and grasped both of her arms, desperate for her to see what a bad idea that was. "I can't put your life in danger again just to find answers. Do you understand that?"

She stared at him, her lips twisting down in a stubborn frown. "I can appreciate that, but I stand by my opinion. I think we need to see what's inside. At least peek into that doorway at the end. This is what we've been looking for."

Thaddeus let out a heavy sigh before taking another step into the tunnel. He shook the framework to test how solid it was. The bars actually felt fairly well built.

Scaffolding, huh? Had someone dragged all these supplies out here just to create this? Had they dug this out using shovels?

He had so many questions.

Maybe it couldn't hurt to go down the tunnel a little to make sure they were on the right track before they sent the police out. After all, what if this proved to be nothing? What if someone had started this tunnel but never completed it?

He let out a sigh. "Let's peek inside. But then we go back and tell Grant so he can handle this."

Miranda held up her phone. "I would call someone now, but, of course, we don't have a signal out here. This island is so patchy when it comes to cell phone service."

"That's what you trade the busy and hectic life in the city for when you come here—for peace and quiet and patchy cell phone service." Thaddeus stared at her, trying to determine if she truly understood what she was getting into. "Are you sure you want to do this?"

After a moment of contemplation, Miranda nodded. "I'm sure. Besides, it's more than curiosity that's driving me. Whoever is behind this wants to hurt us. They're not going to give up. What if we leave the island, and they go after Grant and Abigail?"

She had a point. But Thaddeus wasn't comfortable with her going inside. Still, he had a feeling she was going to go in with or without him. So, he might as well be with her.

"Follow me," he told her. "At the first sign of danger, we turn and go back. Understood?"

"Understood." Miranda nodded.

Apprehension threaded through his muscles as he took another step down the dark tunnel. The scent of stagnant water and stale air surrounded him. He'd seen tunnels like this one other time in his life—when he'd worked at the US/Mexico border.

He pulled up the flashlight on his phone and shone it around so he could see better.

He couldn't imagine the amount of sand that must be on top of this tunnel. If someone had tried to do this with just boards, no doubt they wouldn't have succeeded.

Sand was heavy. The amount on top of them now would likely crush them if the tunnel collapsed.

Thaddeus briefly closed his eyes and lifted a prayer for their safety. He still wasn't sure about this.

Behind him, Miranda clutched his backpack, the action belying her fear. She wasn't as comfortable with this as she tried to make it seem.

Good. Anyone in this situation needed a healthy dose of fear.

"Do you see anything?" she asked.

He shined his light straight ahead and saw what appeared to be a glass doorway about ten or fifteen feet ahead. Relieved it wasn't as far away as he'd thought, he answered, "I can only assume that's the motel."

"This is so crazy. I feel like I'm in an Indiana Jones movie or something."

He smiled at her comparison. "You do love your movie references, don't you?"

"What's that supposed to mean?" Defensiveness edged her voice.

"You quoted several back in Austin also. You just seem awfully sophisticated to be such a movie nerd."

"Just because I like movies doesn't mean I'm a nerd. I can enjoy movies and be sophisticated at the same time."

He brushed cobwebs out of the way, realizing he should have kept his mouth shut. "I didn't mean to imply that. It's just that I can't quite figure you out."

"So you've mentioned."

He paused in front of the door and hesitated as he stared at it.

What would they find on the other side?

Did he really want to know?

Thaddeus already knew the answer to that question.

It was a resounding yes.

MIRANDA COULD HARDLY BREATHE.

She knew this was her idea. She was the one who'd pushed Thaddeus to explore the tunnel. Now that they were in here . . . fear practically swallowed her whole.

She had no idea what could be on the other side of that door. What if more dead bodies were inside?

Or what if the killer was still there?

The unknown only heightened her anxiety.

"Are you sure you don't want to turn back now?" Thaddeus turned toward her and locked his gaze with hers.

Miranda swallowed hard before nodding. "I definitely want to proceed forward."

He pressed his lips together as if second-guessing this decision before finally nodding back.

"Okay then. Let's see what's behind door number one."

Miranda watched as Thaddeus gripped the handle and slowly pulled the door open. A musty scent floated from the other side.

She squeezed closer to Thaddeus, desperate to both see what was inside and to stay safe.

And something about Thaddeus made her feel safe.

She knew she should squash the feeling immediately. Yet she hadn't been able to.

Thaddeus shined his light around.

"This looks like it might have been the lobby at one time." Miranda stepped beside him, one arm still gripping the back of his shirt. She stood entirely too close. She knew she did. But she couldn't back away.

"You're right," Thaddeus muttered. "It does."

One section of roof had partially caved in. A miniature sand dune covered the front desk. Chairs were strewn across the place almost as if an earthquake had struck.

But there were no dead bodies.

That was good news at least, right?

"I think we've confirmed it now." Thaddeus turned back to her. "This is definitely the old motel.

We shouldn't go any farther inside. We don't know how safe this place is. Let's get back to the truck and call for backup. Okay?"

Initially, Miranda thought she'd argue with him. That she'd fight to see more of this place.

But now that she was inside, Thaddeus' words made sense.

It would be unwise to go any further.

The best course of action would be to let law enforcement know and let them proceed from here.

She nodded, not liking how swollen her throat felt. Swollen and clogged with fear. "Okay. Let's get back out there."

They stepped back through the doorway, but as Miranda glanced down the tunnel to the trickle of sunlight that protruded through the vines, she saw movement.

Her lungs froze.

A man wearing all black grabbed the scaffolding and yanked it.

The next instant, sand began to fall . . . collapsing the tunnel.

CHAPTER THIRTY-TWO

THADDEUS KNEW they had no choice but to go back into the motel. Otherwise, they'd be crushed and buried by the sand.

He grabbed Miranda's arm and dove back through the door with her.

Sand immediately filled the tunnel, flooding the space where they'd just been standing.

One of those guys must have seen them in here and decided to finish them off.

Or did they lure them this way?

Thaddeus wouldn't put it past them.

But, now, no one knew Thaddeus and Miranda were down here. No one knew where that tunnel entrance was.

The situation had just gone from bad to worse.

He glanced at Miranda as she sprawled on the ground beside him. "Are you okay?"

She sat up, her face illuminated only by the light on his phone, which had fallen on the floor with the beam pointed up.

She ran a hand over her forehead before nodding. "I think so. But . . ."

With just that one word he heard it. He heard the panic beginning to set in.

That was the last thing that they needed.

His hand covered her arm. "We're going to try to figure out a way out of here."

"But there's no way—"

He cut her off before she could go any further. "We don't know that. There could be more than one entrance that these guys have developed. We need to look for it."

Even as he said the words, he knew that was unlikely. Still, Thaddeus had to give her some hope.

He had brought some water and granola bars with him. They'd have enough to get them through a few days if they were trapped down here. But there were concerns other than food and water.

What was the air supply like down here? Would more of the structure collapse? Were there wild animals who'd made this place a home?

Any number of things could go wrong.

Tears flooded Miranda's eyes. "I am *so* sorry, Thaddeus . . ."

His heart softened when he realized the burden of guilt and grief she must be experiencing. "This was a decision we both made. Don't blame yourself."

"But I'm the one who pushed you to come in here, and now—"

He reached for her again, instinctively touching the side of her neck, cupping her jaw. "Shh. It's going to be okay. Right now, the best thing we can think about is trying to get out of here. We can't change the past, but we can look at the future. Okay?"

Miranda stared at him, unreadable emotions swirling in her gaze. Finally, she broke their connection, looked away, and nodded.

But in that moment, he'd seen the old Miranda, the one he'd been so taken with on that date eight months ago. The vulnerable, down-to-earth girl who seemed like a ringer for the woman of his dreams.

The real Miranda was buried beneath everything else, wasn't she?

What Thaddeus wasn't sure about was why she'd been buried.

But, again, this wasn't the time to figure that out. Right now, they needed to get moving.

Thaddeus pulled himself to his feet and then offered his hand to help her stand. "Let's see what this old place looks like. You have a camera on your phone, right?"

Miranda squinted as if confused. "Yes, but why do I need to take pictures?"

"You're going to want them when you publish the article on this place. Make sure you have it ready."

AS THADDEUS OFFERED Miranda his hand, she gladly accepted it. Her fingers slipped through his, the action feeling natural, like they'd done this a million times before.

Like she'd held hands with Thaddeus, not explored buried motels.

She had to admit his suggestion that she should take pictures was good. Plus, doing so would be a nice distraction for her.

Miranda didn't want to run down the battery of her phone, but it was doing her no good now anyway. Not without any service.

Instead, she snapped a picture of the eerie-looking front desk with the sandy mountains on top and an old tube TV mounted on the wall behind it. This was a place that had been trapped in time.

This piece of history had been preserved right here under an old sand dune. That fact still intrigued her.

Thaddeus crossed the room to a set of glass doors. One had been busted out.

Miranda couldn't figure out where they were in conjunction with the area they'd fallen into through the ceiling. Were they close to it here or was it on the other side of the motel?

She tried to picture Knobs Hill and the layout of the area, but she couldn't.

As Thaddeus opened the door, Miranda slipped inside behind him. A hallway stretched in front of them, with four doors on each side.

Only the beam of the flashlight illuminated the floor for them. She could hardly breathe as she took a step forward.

They stopped at the first room, and Thaddeus paused, his hand hovering over the knob.

Maybe he was nervous also.

It would make him seem more human if he was, and not so much like a superhero.

A superhero? Where had that thought come from?

It didn't matter. Nor did it matter how Thaddeus had looked at her so tenderly when she'd been fighting tears. Or that he had tried his best to distract her from her fear by reminding her to take pictures.

She knew that's what he'd done, and his efforts were touching.

After a moment of hesitation, Thaddeus slowly pushed the door open.

Miranda followed behind him as he crept inside the old motel room.

This one looked much like the one they had landed in, only its condition was better. The space hadn't been damaged quite as much.

They wandered the perimeter, looking for any clues or anything out of place.

Exactly what were they going to find inside this old place?

Miranda wasn't sure. They had a lot more to explore.

But, mostly, she really hoped they found a way out of here.

CHAPTER THIRTY-THREE

THADDEUS CONTINUED to grip Miranda's hand as they searched the rest of the motel. At least this side of it. On the other side of the lobby, he thought there could be another wing.

As they reached the end of the first corridor, he paused by a stairway and glanced up.

"What do you think?" He shined his light up the space.

She shuddered beside him. "I don't think we have much choice at this point. What do we have to lose?"

They had everything to lose, but he didn't tell her that. "We have to watch our steps and be careful. We can't afford for one of us to get hurt right now."

"Agreed." Miranda pressed her lips together as if she didn't like the thought.

"All right, let's do this."

He tested the first step. The wood had more bend to it than he'd like.

"Step only where I step," he told Miranda.

Carefully, they made their way up the staircase until they reached the second floor.

Second floor? Was this the floor they had fallen into? It made sense.

As he took the first step down the hallway, he glanced around, looking for anything to signal which area they should explore next.

Nothing distinguished this place, except for one area where the ceiling had begun to cave in. The sight of it tightened his back muscles.

They really needed to be careful. This whole place was a deathtrap.

But he knew if they were rescued, most likely men would come in from above the dune. That meant it wasn't an option for them to remain on the first floor.

However, depending on how officials decided to get them out of this place—if they even discovered they were down here—heavy machinery could cause this whole place to collapse.

Thaddeus' gut tightened. There were too many unknowns right now for his comfort, too much that could go wrong.

He searched the first room, but there was nothing there. He did the same with the next and the next, continuing farther down the hallway.

As he paused near another room, a crack sounded beneath him.

"Thaddeus?" Miranda said the word with a gasp, as if she realized what was happening a split-second too late.

Before he could react, the floor split open beneath him.

As he began to fall, Miranda's scream filled the air.

———

MIRANDA LUNGED FOR THADDEUS, diving onto her stomach and grabbing his arm near the elbow. She knew she wasn't very strong. But she'd do whatever she could to help.

His legs dangled out of sight, but he'd managed to grab a nearby door frame.

Another crack sounded.

She swerved her head toward the sound and saw that the door molding was coming off the wall.

She scooted closer and gripped his arm more tightly.

"You can't get too close," Thaddeus said through gritted teeth. "The extra weight will cause it to collapse even more."

Miranda froze. He was right.

But how could she help him if she couldn't get any closer?

"Thaddeus . . . what can I do?" Her heart pounded with loud thumps against her chest.

He grimaced as he continued to grip the edge of the doorway. "I'm not sure."

"Maybe I can help pull you back up."

"Or I'll take you down with me."

She ignored the flash of fear at the thought. "I can do this. That door frame is going to split any moment. You need something else to hold onto."

He stared at her as if contemplating his options. He didn't have much time, and she didn't want to remind him of that, but she might have to.

The next instant, he released the door frame with one hand and grabbed her outstretched arm. Miranda held onto his arm with both of hers, determined not to let him go.

As another crack sounded, she sucked in a breath. Would the floor continue to collapse?

Thaddeus grunted as he tried to pull himself back up. His other hand still gripped the door frame, using it as leverage.

Miranda scooted back, desperate to pull him forward.

Finally, Thaddeus moved forward an inch or two.

That was all he needed to get the bulk of his weight above the opening.

He wiggled forward.

The next instant, his legs appeared, and he rolled from the hole onto the floor.

Wasting no time, he scrambled toward her.

He turned and pulled himself upright and leaned back against the wall, his breathing laborious. Letting out a deep breath, he ran a hand over his face.

"That was a close one," he muttered.

Miranda crawled across the floor and paused in front of him, worry still consuming her. He might be out of that hole, but was he really okay?

"Are you hurt?" Miranda quickly looked him up and down, searching for any signs of injury.

She didn't see anything. No blood or protruding bones.

"I'm fine." Thaddeus' gaze caught with hers. "Thank you."

"Maybe we should just take a breather for a moment." She paused beside him and leaned against the wall, still trying to catch her breath. Her heart raced out of control as she realized how badly that could have turned out. "What do you think?"

Thaddeus let out another long breath and closed his eyes. "Maybe that's a good idea."

CHAPTER THIRTY-FOUR

THADDEUS PULLED a granola bar from his backpack and handed half of it to Miranda.

When he saw the concern in her gaze earlier, he had to admit that it touched him.

Miranda had been willing to do whatever it took to help him. That said a lot about her kindness and proved her depth of character.

"I think I know what that guy wanted from us when he came to Abigail's house," she muttered.

He quickly glanced at her, her words taking him by surprise. "What's that?"

Miranda reached into her backpack and pulled out something. "This."

She held up the papers she'd taken from the box

they'd found. She'd already showed them to him once.

"Why would he want those papers? And why did you bring them with you?"

"I wondered if the map might help us when we were out here," she explained. "But I've been thinking. I know we don't know the significance of these. But I wonder if these were plans for a robbery of some sort. That maybe this is a list of names of victims or something. That they were using this place to help plan their crimes."

He cautiously listened to her theory. "I'm not familiar enough with the area to know if there have been a lot of break-ins around here. But just looking at the layout of the building on this sheet, it doesn't strike me as a house. That's one big room and a lot of really small rooms around the perimeter."

"I know. And I have an idea." She paused and nibbled on her lip, almost appearing nervous.

He took another bite of his granola bar. "What's that?"

"Don't laugh at me."

"I won't."

She nibbled on her lip again before saying, "When we were talking to Jared, I heard the news on in the background. The anchor was saying something about a rash of bank robberies in this area of Eastern North Carolina."

"I think I heard something about that also. None here on Cape Corral because I don't think Cape Corral even has a bank. But why do you think these guys are bank robbers? It's not like we found a stash of money."

"The police believe three men are involved . . . maybe only two now, if they're including the dead guy. Anyway, Jared also said those people on the boat had been spotted about five times. Well, there have been four or five bank robberies around here."

As Thaddeus listened to Miranda, he couldn't deny that her words made sense. "I definitely think it's something worth exploring. Can I see the papers again?"

She handed them to him, and he examined the drawings with Miranda's theory in mind. "This *could* be a bank."

Excitement lit her gaze. "And that list of names? Could they be bank executives maybe?"

"Why would these guys need the names of bank executives?"

She shrugged. "I don't know. Maybe so they could research them. Find leverage on them. Watch them and learn their schedules."

Thaddeus wished he had service down here because Miranda's theory had his blood racing. More than anything, he wanted to call and follow up with this to see if Miranda was correct. Her theory had some merit.

He glanced at her and slowly nodded. "I'm impressed. Good job."

She blushed as she glanced away and said, "Thank you."

The woman he was looking at now was the woman he'd met on that date back in Austin.

The one Thaddeus could see himself falling in love with.

Was this the real Miranda?

He wanted to say that it was.

But his walls refused to come down.

Because what if he was wrong . . . again?

MIRANDA SAW SOMETHING CHANGE IN THADDEUS' gaze. What exactly was he thinking? Was this a good time to ask him?

She wasn't sure. She only knew that there were many layers to Thaddeus—layers that still made her incredibly curious.

She rubbed her lips together, tempted to ask more questions and trying not to bask too much in his praise.

But before anything left her lips, Thaddeus shrugged into his backpack again. "We should keep looking and see if we can find the original area we fell through. If anyone comes to look for us, that's the most likely place they'll go. I'm sure that Grant somehow pinned the general location on his phone as we were looking for the hole, so it will be the easiest to find."

Miranda quickly scrambled to her feet and nodded. "That makes sense."

"We're going to have to go farther down this hall-way. But we need to be careful and watch our every step. We can't have another replay of what just happened."

Her throat felt dry at the words as she glanced at the dark space. "I understand."

"You sure you're okay with this?" He leveled his gaze with hers.

"I'm sure." Even as she said the words, Miranda was anything but sure. But she had no other choice right now.

"Just like on the stairway, step only where I step, okay?"

"Okay."

There were just four more doorways they needed to check down this hallway. Hopefully when they got past this unstable area, they'd be safe.

She pressed herself against the wall, trying to stay as far away from the hole as possible. Her first instinct was to leap across it, but she knew that that wouldn't be safe either. It would be too much weight all at once on the wood. That kind of impact could cause it to crack and break further.

As Thaddeus paused outside the next room, Miranda held her breath, wondering what exactly they would find inside.

As he opened the door, she followed the beam of his flashlight.

This was the same room they'd discovered when they were trapped inside this place earlier, she realized.

The one with a dead body.

But as Miranda's gaze went to the space behind the dresser, she saw the dead body was now gone.

CHAPTER THIRTY-FIVE

THADDEUS FELT his jaw tighten as he stared at the empty space behind that old dresser. "These guys came back, took the body, and probably buried it somewhere else."

"Why would these guys go through all that trouble?"

"They were probably afraid the police would come and find it. That body could have offered more evidence as to what was going on—as well as given the police the chance to charge someone with murder."

"But Grant already thought he'd identified the body."

"These guys don't know that. If we know for sure

the identity of this person, then we might find more answers."

Carefully, Thaddeus walked across the room and opened the door to the area he and Miranda had fallen into.

He stared at the space that had once been a hole leading to the dune above. Sand had caved in and now covered almost the entire space beneath it.

For a moment, Thaddeus wondered if they could climb the sand and try somehow to dig out.

But he knew the sand would continue to fall on them and could ultimately lead to their demise. They couldn't risk that.

At least, they couldn't risk it right now. Maybe as a last resort.

Thaddeus still held onto the hope that Grant and his crew would find them.

As he glanced around, he realized all they could do right now was wait.

"What are you thinking?" Miranda's soft voice sounded beside him.

"I'm thinking we should sit down and make ourselves comfortable for a few minutes." As he spoke, he pulled a battery-powered lantern from his backpack and set it up between them. He switched off his phone and slid it back in his pocket. "We have some time to kill before we take any more action."

He hoped that decision didn't get them hurt. But he was fresh out of ideas on what else to do.

———

THE ONLY THING Miranda hated more than not doing anything was waiting.

As she glanced at Thaddeus in front of her, her nerves kicked in.

She'd been avoiding asking him hard questions because she thought she might get hurt. But after this wedding was over, the two of them would probably never see each other again. Why not ask him some questions?

She had nothing to lose.

"Why didn't you call me?" she blurted as she pulled her jeans-clad legs to her chest.

His eyebrows shot in the air. "After our date?"

She gave him a look. "Yes, after our date. I thought we'd really connected."

"We did. But then literally that same evening is when everything went down with my partner. I got swept up in something I didn't know if I'd ever get out of. The whole situation pretty much consumed me. That doesn't mean I didn't think about you. The timing was just terrible."

Miranda frowned and nibbled on her lip for a moment. She supposed his explanation made sense. But, still, she wasn't ready to just let this go.

"What about afterward?" she pushed. "Once some of the storm passed? Did you ever think about contacting me then?"

Thaddeus hesitated before answering. "Did I think about it? I did more than think about seeing you. I was on leave of absence from the bureau, so I decided to surprise you and visit you in New York."

Her heart beat harder at his words as confusion gripped her. "Really? But . . ."

His expression remained somber. "When I got there, I went to your office building to surprise you."

"How did you even know where I worked?"

"I checked your social media profile. Anyway, before I could even ask the receptionist for you, I saw you walk out to meet another man. This guy kissed you on the cheek, and you guys looked awfully happy together."

"Brian . . ." she muttered.

"It seemed like you'd moved on. Or maybe you'd been dating him all along."

Her head started to pound. "No, actually we'd

just started dating. But I didn't hear from you for two weeks, and then I met Brian. He asked me out, and I figured the best way to get over your rejection was by saying yes. I'm pretty sure, if I understand what you're telling me correctly, that right about the time you came to visit me would have been near one of our first dates."

"Well, you guys looked pretty cozy."

"I don't know what to say. He probably just kissed me on the cheek as a greeting. If I'd known that you were there . . . I wouldn't have seen Brian anymore. My roommate kept insisting that I didn't give guys a chance, so I decided I should see what would happen between Brian and me. I thought I'd see if he measured up to . . . you."

Surprise rushed through Thaddeus' gaze. "Really?"

"Really. I wish you had talked to me."

He glanced away, and, when he did, Miranda knew that there was more to this story.

"I did think about reaching out to show you that I wanted to get to know you more."

"I have a feeling there's a but in there . . ."

His gaze met hers. "I don't know how to say this so I'm just going to come right out with it and not mince words. The woman I saw in New York seemed nothing like the woman I met in Texas. She appeared high-maintenance and self-important and . . . dating someone else. It was like you were a completely different person."

Miranda felt the blood drain from her face. How could she even explain to Thaddeus the change in her? What could she say?

Then she remembered again that she really had nothing to lose right now.

She licked her lips as she prepared herself to dive in again.

CHAPTER THIRTY-SIX

THADDEUS WATCHED as Miranda seemed to try to put together her thoughts. He didn't rush her or pressure her. If she had something else to say, he would listen.

But he was glad they'd been able to get this off their chests. The situation between them had remained unspoken for entirely too long. That was partially his fault also.

"The truth is, I feel like I'm caught between two worlds, and I don't know what to do about it." Her voice sounded strained as she said the words.

"What do you mean?"

She glanced in the distance, a far-off look in her eyes. This conversation obviously was causing her some stress.

"I've always been the studious, quiet bookworm who liked nature, who didn't mind getting dirty, who can quote favorite movies, and I'm not ashamed on occasion to even engage in some cosplay. I'm okay with who I am. But when I started applying for the jobs I really wanted in New York, I wasn't getting them despite the fact that I had the credentials. That's when I realized that being a mousy, nerdy girl wasn't going to cut it."

"You're going to have to spell that out some more for me."

"In New York, it seems like there's a certain image that goes with being successful, and, after a while, I learned I had to live up to that image if I wanted to succeed. It's not that I wanted to be fake. Not at all. But it's just a different world than the one I came from in Ohio. My roommate helped give me a makeover. My hair was suddenly blonde. Makeup covered my imperfections. I traded my glasses for contacts and my thrift store finds for designer duds."

"So, you basically transformed yourself in order to further your career?" As much as Thaddeus appreciated the explanation, he wasn't sure he understood Miranda any more than he had originally.

"I know it probably doesn't make sense. But I

had to try to make a go of it. I figured changing the way I dressed was really just a method to succeed. To be honest, I don't love the job like I thought I would. I don't love the maintenance of keeping up appearances. That's why I want to find a different job so badly. I want to get out of that scene and find myself again."

Thaddeus listened, trying to process her revelation.

Miranda dragged her gaze to meet his. "I know how this might sound and look. But what I told you is the truth. Honestly, I wouldn't blame you if you didn't believe me. But these are the lessons I've had to learn, maybe even learn the hard way."

Thaddeus swallowed hard as he tried to find the right words. "I appreciate your honesty. It takes a strong person to admit what you're going through."

She shrugged, her gaze still appearing burdened. "I don't feel like a strong person. I feel like I should have things figured out. But the truth of the matter is that I don't. But if there's one thing that facing death has taught me, it's that life is too short to live for other people. When we get out of this situation, I'm going to make some changes. Because how often is a person given a second chance to make things right?"

MIRANDA WASN'T sure if she should feel self-conscious after her admission or not. But she felt surprisingly refreshed to get that out in the open.

For as long as she could remember, men had abandoned her.

Her dad had left when she was only two, and she hadn't heard from him since. Her first boyfriend had broken up with her when he met someone more attractive. Then there was Brian, who'd left her in the drugstore in the middle of an armed robbery.

So, of course, it was natural that she'd assumed Thaddeus had abandoned her also.

But he'd actually come to New York . . .

Her heart thumped in her ears. If Miranda had known that it would have changed so much. Maybe things would have never blown up with Brian like they had.

If her mental timeline was correct, she'd only gone out on one date with Brian when Thaddeus had come to town.

She'd thought about asking Abigail if she knew what was going on with Thaddeus at the time. But Miranda hadn't wanted to drag her friends into the middle of it. She'd also thought about calling Thaddeus herself. After all, she was a modern-day woman.

Yet she didn't want to be the pursuer in the relationship. Maybe some people would call her old-fashioned, but she wanted the man to chase her.

"What happened with your partner?" she asked quietly.

He took his hat off and set it beside him, his gaze suddenly burdened. "That night, after our date, he called me. Said he needed help. I went out to a ranch in the area to meet him. When I got there, it was too late. He'd been shot."

"That's terrible."

"He was still alive. I called 911 and tried to stop his bleeding, even though . . ." His voice cracked. "Even though I knew I was too late. Anyway," he drew in a deep breath, "the last thing he said to me was Simpson."

"What did that mean?" Miranda could hardly breathe as she waited for him to continue.

"Simpson was another FBI agent, one I didn't particularly care for. I couldn't put my finger on why, but I knew if Hoffer said her name, there was a reason." He ran his hand over his face.

Miranda waited, giving him time to collect his thoughts.

"By the time my partner got to the hospital, he was gone," Thaddeus continued. "Afterward, I set out to figure out exactly what happened, and I discovered that Simpson was playing both sides. A local rancher had her in his pocket and was paying her to look the other way and destroy any reports coming in about the illegal activities happening on his property."

"That's awful."

He nodded, the action heavy and labored. "I collected all the evidence I could, but she discovered what I was doing and put out a hit on me. Eventually, I convinced my superior what was going on. Long story short, she was arrested. I was given mandatory leave of absence to recover from everything that happened."

"And that's when you came to New York . . ."

He nodded.

"I'm so sorry, Thaddeus. I had no idea."

"I know. I'm still trying to figure things out, to be honest. I worked my whole adult life to get where I am, only to discover that maybe it's not what I want at all. There's too much bureaucracy. Too much red tape, you know?"

"Yeah, I know." His words reflected, in many ways, her own feelings.

All she'd wanted was to get a job at a top New York magazine.

But the position was nothing like she'd thought it would be.

Thaddeus glanced at her in the dim light, the shadows moving across his face only making him look more alluring. "I just want you to know that when we went out, it was one of the best nights of my life."

Miranda's eyebrows shot up. She hadn't expected his statement.

She smiled as she remembered their date. "That was one of the best nights for me too."

"I knew on our date when it started raining and you insisted on staying outside on that rock to watch the storm that you're pretty amazing."

"I've never really minded getting wet in the rain. Unless I'm in New York, and I've just had my hair blown out." She offered a weak smile that quickly faded. "I guess it's too bad that we can't go back for a do-over, huh?"

"Yeah, I guess it is." His voice sounded as somber as her own.

Strained silence hung between them.

Finally, Miranda glanced at her watch. "It's already past nine. Can you believe that?"

"Maybe the best thing we can do is get some rest and start fresh in the morning. I'm hoping Grant will be able to look for us and find us early tomorrow."

"Me too." Her voice came out just above a whisper.

As she sat in the middle of the room, Miranda realized she wasn't going to be able to rest in this position. Thaddeus patted the spot beside him, and she quickly scooted toward him.

His arm went around her, and she rested her head against him.

She wasn't sure how much sleep she'd get tonight. But Miranda felt much better by Thaddeus' side.

CHAPTER THIRTY-SEVEN

THADDEUS WAS FAIRLY certain Miranda was sleeping. Her chest rose and fell at an even pace, and her head seemed limp against his chest.

He hadn't expected to share that story about Hoffer. About the betrayal he'd felt at the hands of another FBI agent. But it felt good to get it off his chest.

All these months later, he was still recovering. Still trying to figure out what he wanted to do with his future.

He didn't believe in running away from his troubles. But he couldn't help but think that maybe a change would be good for him.

He held Miranda closer as regret clutched him.

All these months he'd blamed her for not being the person he'd thought. But now he realized he shared the blame for what had happened between them.

Instead of having a conversation, he'd jumped to more than one conclusion. That response had been wrong. Sure, he could blame everything that happened back in Austin for his lack of clear thinking. After what happened with Hoffer, he had been consumed with grief.

The one thing he'd been looking forward to was seeing Miranda again. Then when it hadn't worked out as he'd expected . . . he'd made assumptions.

Was it too late to make things right?

He wasn't sure.

But still the question remained: even if the two of them did pursue a relationship, they lived several states away from each other.

Her job was in New York and Thaddeus' was in Texas. Not only that, but he had no desire to move to New York. He wasn't sure if she could do her job in Texas.

Maybe the signs had been in front of him the whole time—signs that a relationship between them wouldn't work.

But Thaddeus also knew that when a person

found something special that they shouldn't take that for granted.

As Miranda pulled in a deep breath, he turned toward her and placed a gentle kiss on the top of her head.

He wasn't sure what would be next for them—if anything.

He wasn't even sure about his own future.

But, right now, his biggest concern needed to be getting out of this place alive.

The only way they were going to do that was if Grant found them.

MIRANDA AWOKE with a start and found herself in Thaddeus' arms.

She pulled back, not realizing she'd been sleeping so soundly.

How could she sleep so deeply in these circumstances? It didn't even make sense.

Thaddeus didn't seem shaken at all as she straightened her back and turned toward him.

In fact, he looked wide awake without even a hint of sleepiness in his gaze.

"Good morning," he muttered.

"Good morning." Miranda ran a hand over her face, hoping she didn't have drool or the impression of his shirt on the side of her face. "Did you get any sleep?"

"No, not really. Too much on my mind."

She glanced around the space, at once remembering where they were.

Fear instantly filled her lungs until she could hardly breathe.

That's right. She and Thaddeus were trapped. Without a way out.

And it was all her fault. She should have never suggested coming in here.

Had she always let her career dictate her life choices?

Looking back, she couldn't deny she had.

But that needed to change.

She was tired of trying to be someone else just so she could be successful.

And she should have never put Thaddeus' life at risk just because she wanted a change in her own life. It had been selfish and foolish.

"Granola bar?" He held one up to her.

Miranda shook her head, her stomach uneasy. "I'm okay."

"You need to keep your energy level up."

"Maybe later."

She raked her hands through her hair as she glanced around. Thaddeus had already turned on the small lantern, which illuminated only a few feet around them.

"If Grant and his crew were above us right now, do you think we could hear them?" Miranda asked.

"That's a good question. I want to say yes, but considering we could potentially have three feet of sand above us . . . I'm not sure." Thaddeus rose to his feet and stretched before walking toward the other room.

"Where are you going?" she rushed, trying to ignore the impulse of panic.

"I had an idea I thought might help us get out of here with air in our lungs instead of sand. I could use a hand."

"Of course." Miranda scrambled to her feet. "Anything."

She watched as Thaddeus searched through the rubbish in the other room. Finally, he grabbed a headboard.

"I think we need to lift this as high as we can until we can push it out of the sand on the other side. It'll be a good marker when someone comes to find us."

Her mind raced as she processed his words. "Do you think we could just dig out?"

"I thought about it all night, but I'm afraid the sand would cover us and make the situation worse." He shrugged. "If I know Grant, he won't stop looking until he finds us."

"But does he even know we're down here? What if he thinks we went to Nags Head or something?"

"I think he knows us well enough to know there's a good chance we came back this way. He'll look for his truck, and, when he realizes where it is, I'm hoping this is the next conclusion he draws."

Another thought slammed into her mind. "The rehearsal dinner is tonight. What kind of celebration is it going to be if both of their best friends are dead?"

"Don't think like that." Thaddeus stepped closer and pushed her hair out of her eyes.

Miranda froze. Every inch of her went on alert, from her heart all the way to her fingertips.

Thaddeus stood close enough to kiss her.

She wondered what it would be like to relive that kiss they'd shared in Austin.

Miranda wet her lips at the thought of it.

She'd be lying if she denied her desire to feel his lips against hers again. She wanted to know if she'd still feel that same spark between them.

But instead of leaning into a kiss, Thaddeus stepped back and cleared his throat. "Grab the other side of this headboard."

Disappointment hit Miranda like a bulldozer.

She released the breath she'd been holding and stepped back, hoping the emotion didn't show on her face.

She'd thought Thaddeus was feeling the same thing she was. But she'd been wrong . . . again.

It was better this way. All they needed to focus on right now was survival . . . about not being buried in this oversized coffin in the ground. Her love life was the least of her concerns. Or, rather, it should be.

They carried the headboard back to the mound of sand that now engulfed the room.

"It isn't going to be easy, and I don't know exactly how deep the sand is." Thaddeus studied a spot on the floor. "But if we could just push the headboard up through the sand . . ."

"I'll give it everything I've got," Miranda told him.

He nodded before shoving it up into the mound

of sand and balancing it on his shoulder. As he did, Miranda placed her palms on the other side of it also. Then on the count of three, they thrust upward.

But as they did, more sand began filling the room —at a rapid pace.

CHAPTER THIRTY-EIGHT

THADDEUS GRABBED Miranda's arm and jerked her back before the sand could consume her.

The grains dumped inside fast enough to bury them.

They darted into the other room and paused, watching until the cascade ended.

At least half of the room was now covered.

Miranda stepped closer to him, her motions stiff with fear. "Do you think we got the headboard up high enough?"

Thaddeus stared at the mound and frowned. "It's hard to say. But let's hope so."

"I guess until then we just wait."

He glanced around, wondering if there was any

evidence he'd missed. At this point, he hardly even cared. All he wanted was to get out of here.

Even though he knew that there was enough air in this room to breathe, his lungs still felt incredibly tight.

"We're going to get out of here." Miranda squeezed his forearm. "I will not ruin my best friend's wedding. I won't."

He let out a long breath and lifted his cowboy hat, raking a hand through his hair. "You're right. We are going to get out. If Grant doesn't come find us, then we'll just keep searching until we figure out another way."

As he said the words, Thaddeus thought he heard a sound above them.

He couldn't be sure, but it almost sounded like . . . voices.

Miranda glanced above her, her eyes widening.

She'd heard the noise too.

Maybe someone was above them.

Before he missed an opportunity, he cupped his hands around his lips and began to yell, "Down here! We're down here!"

Miranda joined him, shouting as loud as she could.

Then they paused and waited to see what happened next.

AT LEAST THIRTY minutes had passed since they'd first heard the noise above them.

Miranda *thought* she heard people talking. Maybe even movement. But it was so hard to know for sure.

Part of her waited in anticipation, fearing the whole ceiling would collapse. Another part let her hope soar, praying that unleashing that optimism didn't make it even more painful if they weren't rescued.

What if the people who'd trapped them in here came back? What if the people they heard weren't their rescuers but the people who wanted to kill them?

A soft cry escaped from her lips at the thought.

"Hey . . ." Thaddeus said.

When she looked over at him, he tugged her toward him and folded his arms around her in a hug.

"It's going to be okay," he murmured.

She melted in his embrace. Having someone to

hold her up felt so good and made her realize exactly what she was missing in her life—a strong support system filled with people who wouldn't let her down.

Throughout this entire situation, Thaddeus hadn't let her down. He'd always been there when Miranda needed him. When she was in danger, he hadn't turned his back on her.

That fact hadn't gone unnoticed.

She remained in his embrace, unable to bring herself to move from the safety of his arms.

Until a beam of light hit them.

Miranda sucked in a breath and looked up just in time to see a shovel break through the roof in the other room.

"What . . . ?" she muttered.

Thaddeus turned, his gaze fastened on the scene also.

A few minutes later, Grant's face appeared.

They'd been found!

Thaddeus let out a whoop before pulling her into his arms and twirling her around. "We're going to get out of here!"

Miranda laughed with a mix of relief and joy. "Yes, we are."

She couldn't believe it. She actually might get out of this place and be able to give life another chance.

CHAPTER THIRTY-NINE

"AFTER YOU WENT MISSING, we were able to rush the permit," Grant explained as Thaddeus and Miranda stood atop Knobs Hill with him.

A whole crew was on the scene—police, fire, rescue.

An excavator sat near the base of the dune, and shovels were scattered across the sand from where rescuers had been searching.

In the distance, the sun had risen over the water and shone on them with favor.

Thaddeus turned back to his friend. "I'm glad you found us when you did. I'm not sure how much longer we would have survived down there considering the conditions. How did you know that's where we were?"

Grant shrugged. "It was our best guess. But when I found my truck parked on the edge of Wash Woods, it made sense. What I'm still not sure about is how you guys got in."

Thaddeus and Miranda filled in the details. In between their statements, they took sips of water that had been handed to them. Miranda kept a blanket around her shoulders to ward off the slight chill in the air.

A crew secured the area so the motel could be safely investigated. But Thaddeus had already told Grant that the body was now missing. He also shared their theory about the bank robberies.

"Do you know anything about them?" Thaddeus asked.

Grant let out a breath. "I know that authorities are still trying to figure out how these guys are getting past the alarm systems unnoticed."

"What about Bobby Joe?" Miranda blurted.

Thaddeus and Grant turned toward her and waited for her to continue.

"You think the dead man with the tattoo was Bobby Joe, right?" she asked.

Grant nodded. "We do."

"You said he installed security systems at area

businesses. Did he install the systems at these banks?"

Grant twisted his neck in thought. "That's definitely a theory worth exploring. That would clear up a lot of questions now, wouldn't it?"

"I'd say," Thaddeus agreed.

"I'll look into it. In the meantime, I'm glad you two are okay. That could have turned out really ugly."

"I know." Miranda frowned and pulled the blanket at her shoulders tighter. "I'm sorry this happened on the day before your wedding. I hate to see you working right now when you should be enjoying yourself."

"Levi will be back today to take over. I'm going to work right up until the rehearsal. Abigail is a saint and said she understands. My hands are kind of tied at this point."

Grant was fortunate that his fiancée was so understanding. But, like Miranda, Thaddeus also wished the timing on all this wasn't so awful.

"If there's anything we can do to help, you just let us know," Thaddeus said.

"Will do. In the meantime, why don't you two get back to Abigail's and get showered? You're both looking a little rough."

Thaddeus glanced at Miranda and saw the dirt smudging her cheeks and nose. Her mussed hair made her look like she'd just awakened. Her clothes were stained and wrinkled.

But she still looked gorgeous.

Thaddeus pressed his lips together as he felt something beginning to grow inside him.

"Fire Chief Dillion McGrath said he would take you back to the truck so you can drive to Abigail's," Grant continued. "He's waiting over there."

Before they headed toward him, Miranda paused. "By the way, I'm sorry about the bullet holes at Abigail's place. It seems I have a lot to apologize for."

"You have nothing to be sorry about," Grant said. "Dash told me everything that happened. We have someone coming over today to patch everything up, and the house will be as good as new before we know it."

With a nod, Thaddeus and Miranda took off toward Fire Chief McGrath.

Thaddeus' thoughts remained on the scene. He would have stayed . . . if he thought he could convince Miranda not to get involved.

But the best thing he could do right now was to stay close . . . her life might depend on it.

AFTER RETURNING TO THE HOUSE, the rest of the day was a whirlwind.

By the time Miranda chatted a few minutes with Abigail and then hopped in the shower, the rest of the bridesmaids had arrived. Apparently, Emmy's fiancé had picked them up at the airport and brought them here.

The rest of the afternoon was filled with manicures and facials and getting their hair done.

Miranda tried to operate as if nothing were wrong—even though everything felt wrong.

She couldn't stop thinking about Thaddeus. About their talk. About what he was doing right now.

If she had to guess, he'd gone back to the scene with Grant to investigate.

At five, Levi Sutherland arrived to personally escort all the ladies to the church for the wedding rehearsal.

On the drive there, guilt pressed on Miranda as she realized how much she'd done to detract from her best friend's big day.

None of it had been intentional. Still, she

couldn't help but feel bad, even though Abigail had shown the utmost grace.

When she stepped inside the church, her gaze went to the stage. Thaddeus stood there in jeans, a white button-up shirt, and a Stetson.

Miranda's heart skipped a beat at the sight of him. He looked so incredibly handsome. Like the man of her dreams, for that matter. The one who'd protected her with his life and made her feel like the most important person in the world.

As she remembered their heart-to-heart talk last night, she couldn't help but wonder: Could the two of them have a second chance?

Was it possible that their time away from each other had been necessary so they could learn about themselves and figure out what they really wanted?

Even if that was true, what would their future even look like?

As Miranda lingered at the back of the building, she realized she wasn't sure.

But she hoped that sometime before they left, the two of them would have a chance to talk about it.

"You ready?" Abigail asked, motioning for Miranda to follow her so the wedding coordinator could dole out instructions.

Miranda pulled herself from her daze and nodded. "Of course."

But her mind continued to race through everything that had happened. She only prayed that nothing else would happen to distract from Grant and Abigail's big day.

Especially not anything of the dangerous variety.

CHAPTER FORTY

THADDEUS COULDN'T WAIT to have a moment alone with Miranda.

He couldn't take his eyes off her at the rehearsal.

She'd smoothed her honey-blonde hair into soft curls. Applied some light makeup. Wore a flowered navy-blue dress that showed her tiny waist.

She looked amazing.

She *was* amazing.

But he needed the chance to tell her that.

The group waited outside after the rehearsal to catch rides together to the dinner, which would take place back at Abigail's. Caterers had arrived to set up while they were at the rehearsal, from what Thaddeus understood.

As Miranda paced away from the rest of the

bridesmaids, her gaze distracted, he knew he had his chance to talk.

"Hey, you," he called.

She paused and turned toward him, crossing her arms as she grinned. "Hey, yourself."

Darkness hung around them, and, in the distance, he could hear the waves crashing in the ocean.

The church was in a fairly secluded part of the island, and a patch of woods sprouted on the other side of the building, beside a graveyard that had seen better days.

"You look really lovely, Miranda."

Miranda touched a curl that cascaded over her shoulder. "Thank you. You look awfully nice yourself."

He leaned closer, knowing he didn't have any time to waste. Too much time had already been plundered. "Listen, I've been thinking. I don't want any type of misunderstanding to cause hard feelings between us."

"I don't either." She nibbled on her lip a moment before stepping closer. "I'm glad we had the chance to reconnect."

"I am too." As Thaddeus stared down at her, something ignited inside him.

He'd been a fool to let Miranda get away once. He couldn't let that happen again.

He reached for her neck and cupped his hand beneath her jaw. Gently, he ran his thumb along the edge of her face before stopping at her lips.

Miranda went still, almost seeming as if she weren't breathing.

The next instant, he leaned forward, and his lips covered hers. She leaned into him, bending into his arms as her hands reached for his neck.

Suddenly, it was like he'd been transported back in time. Back to that evening in Austin.

Only this time, the kiss was even better. Even sweeter. Even deeper.

He pulled away, trying to let his thoughts regroup. But his arms remained around her waist. He couldn't bring himself to let go.

"What are we going to do?" she murmured. "What does all of this even mean?"

He leaned his forehead into hers. "We need to figure that out. But I know what I want."

Miranda held her breath as if waiting for whatever else he had to say.

THADDEUS SWALLOWED HARD, trying to find the right words.

"You really think we can make this work between us?" Miranda murmured.

"I do. I enjoy being with this version of you." He kept his forehead gently resting on hers. "The woman I had such a great time with in Austin."

She withdrew slightly. "What do you mean *this version?*"

"I just mean . . . you seemed like a different person when I saw you in New York City." As soon as he said the words, he knew they weren't coming out right, but he wasn't sure how to correct himself.

"You mean the version of Miranda that you didn't even bother to talk to? The one you assumed was nothing like the version you'd met in Austin?"

"What was I supposed to think? You're the one who admitted you had a makeover to become someone you're not. Are you going to return to being that person in New York?"

She stepped out of his embrace, fire lighting her gaze. "There are no two versions of me. If you'd approached me in New York, you would've seen right through to the person I am. You would've recognized that I was still me, deep down."

"Would I?"

Pain seared through her gaze, along with another healthy dose of anger. "After I explained to you why I did what I did, you're still making assumptions? You still think I was pretending when I was with you on our date?"

Thaddeus bit down, trying to choose his words carefully. He had a feeling that no matter what he said it would sound wrong. "I . . . I don't know what to think anymore."

"All along, you've felt like this misunderstanding between us was my fault when, in fact, it was just as much yours. You never bothered to ask me what the truth was."

"Because I thought you were dating someone else and it would be inappropriate! I'm not the guy who's going to steal you away from another guy. I thought you'd made your choice."

"I hadn't! You just made too many assumptions!"

"And you didn't? You just assumed when you didn't hear from me right away that I pretended to like you on our date. That I was just in it for the one night? That that kiss we shared meant nothing to me. That I had moved on without so much as calling you."

Miranda opened her mouth. Then snapped it shut.

The two of them stared at each other, an invisible wall shooting up between them.

For a brief moment, she'd thought the two of them were on the same page. But it turned out they weren't. Not even close.

As Thaddeus heard a stick crack behind them, he turned.

A tall man with dark hair stood at the edge of the woods.

"Mars Jensen?" Miranda's jaw went slack as she stared at the man. "What are you doing here?"

"The two of us need to have a talk," the man growled. "Alone."

CHAPTER FORTY-ONE

THADDEUS THOUGHT the man's name seemed familiar, but he didn't know why.

All Thaddeus knew was that this guy appeared dangerous. His shifting gaze, brooding stance, and clenched fists said it all.

He quickly pulled Miranda behind him. Their fight no longer mattered. Keeping Miranda safe was the only thing important right now.

"You're not getting anywhere near her," Thaddeus said.

"I've been watching you." The man ignored Thaddeus' statement, his eyes on Miranda.

"*You're* the one who's been following me?" Miranda's voice sounded breathless as she stared at the man. "Leaving me messages?"

"That's right. I wanted to dig up dirt on you, just like you dug up dirt on me." He practically spit the words out, yet they still somehow sounded slurred. The man's gaze seemed off-balance and his actions almost manic.

"She dug up dirt on you?" Thaddeus repeated. "Wait . . . who are you?"

"Mars Jenson, the world-famous golfer who took home three gold medals at the Olympics," Miranda explained. "I did a feature article on him a couple of months ago."

"She ruined my life." Mars' words held venom as he sneered at Miranda.

"How did I ruin your life?" Miranda asked. "All I did was write a profile on you."

"You talked to Shelby Bolster and got a quote from her. I didn't know that was a part of the deal."

"It's not unusual to get quotes from friends and coworkers. It's part of my job."

"Don't act so innocent. Before your article came out, my wife suspected I was having an affair with Shelby, but I told her I hadn't seen the woman in months. Then you quoted Shelby as saying we met together once every month. My wife read that article. She packed up and left me."

"She did?" Miranda's voice pitched higher. "I'm

sorry to hear that, but it's not my fault. I had no idea she'd draw those conclusions."

"You should have never quoted Shelby for the article!"

"You lied to your wife, got caught, and now you've been following Miranda around hoping for revenge?" Thaddeus repeated. "Are you the who's been shooting at her?"

"Shooting at her?" Mars' thick eyebrows shoved together. "Why would I do that? That would ruin my career on top of everything else I've lost."

"What are you doing, if not that?" Miranda's voice quivered as her question hung in the air.

"I just wanted to send you a message." His words came out biting and sharp.

"You're the one who left that photo on the Jeep."

Mars' eyes gleamed with satisfaction. "I did. I want something to bring you down. To make you hurt the way you hurt me. To remind you that you're not perfect either."

Miranda clutched Thaddeus' arm as she stared at Mars. "I know I'm not perfect. I'm trying to figure out life just like everyone else. I never meant to hurt you. I had no idea there was something between you and Shelby. How would I know that?"

"You should have kept your nose out of my

personal business!" Mars' gaze went to Thaddeus. "Did you know your girlfriend used to be a total geek? The person everyone ignored?"

This guy must have seen him and Miranda together, and something had snapped inside him. It was the only reason he'd revealed himself right now. That . . . and because he wanted to ruin Miranda.

"You need to watch yourself." Thaddeus bristled. "Just because Miranda supposedly tarnished your image doesn't mean you need to try to tarnish hers."

"She doesn't deserve to be happy! Especially not after what she did to me!"

"All she did was tell the truth. She didn't mean to hurt you."

"I looked into Miranda," Mars continued, his eyes full of rage and vengeance. "She was the girl everyone abandoned. It's easy for that to happen when you're an invisible nobody."

Miranda sucked in a breath beside him as if the man's words had been like a slap in the face.

"She's not a nobody," Thaddeus practically growled.

"How did you even find that old photo of me?" Miranda asked. "Find out any of that information?"

"It wasn't hard. A little research did the trick. There was a picture of you in one of your old high school yearbooks—and enough information online that I could put together the complete picture. You'd obviously changed and were ashamed of the person you used to be. I decided to use that to my advantage."

"That's a lot of trouble to go through . . ." Miranda muttered. "And how did you find me here?"

"I ran into one of your coworkers while I was in New York—I'd been watching you, trying to get a better feel for who you were. When I saw you leave for the airport, I just 'happened' to run into a coworker. I told her I wanted to thank you for the article, but she told me you were coming down to Cape Corral for a wedding. From there, it wasn't hard to track you down here."

"You have no right to be here," Thaddeus said. "You have no right to say those things about her."

"Why not? She ruined my life. I'm going to ruin hers." Mars lunged toward them.

As he did, Miranda let out a scream.

MIRANDA SAW MARS charging toward them and braced herself for whatever would happen. She prayed Thaddeus wasn't hurt. That this situation didn't turn deadly.

But before he could reach her, Thaddeus intercepted and shoved the man out of the way.

Mars wobbled and then fell back on the ground.

He'd been drinking, hadn't he? That explained his slurred words. Explained why he'd confronted her now of all times.

He climbed back to his unsteady feet and lunged at Thaddeus again.

But Thaddeus was ready and bristled. As soon as the man touched him, he grabbed his arm and twisted it behind him. With one swift move, he had the man facedown on the ground.

"Hey! What's going on here?" Levi rushed outside and toward them. He pulled out his handcuffs and grabbed Mars.

"He tried to assault Miranda."

"Oh, yeah?" Levi snapped the cuffs on Mars. "You're under arrest."

Mars tried to jerk out of Levi's grasp, but Levi held tight.

"I didn't do anything." Mars' nostrils flared with anger. "Don't you know who I am? I'm an Olympic gold medalist. I'm important! Not like this nobody who ruined my life! You should arrest her."

"He's the one who has been following me. Leaving the threatening messages," Miranda's voice shook as she said the words.

Levi pulled the man to his feet. "Harassment, stalking, leaving threats . . . not to mention attempted assault. All reasons you're going to jail."

"You have no proof I did any of that." Mars slurred the words through gritted teeth.

"Miranda, did you save any of those threats you received?" Levi glanced at her.

She nodded, her mind still swirling over what had just happened. "As a matter of fact, I did. All of them."

"Great. Bring them by the station when you have the chance."

"Of course."

"Now, you two go ahead and get to the rehearsal dinner." Levi nodded toward the vehicles waiting in the distance. "I know everyone is waiting for you. I'll handle this guy."

Mars muttered curses beneath his breath as he glared at them.

As they walked away, Miranda looked up at Thaddeus. What did she even say after all that? One moment, he'd been kissing her like no one but

Thaddeus had ever kissed her. The next instant, they were at each other's throats.

She finally settled on pushing a hair behind her ear and murmuring, "Thank you."

"Of course."

They stared at each other another moment until finally Miranda pointed over her shoulder. "We should get going."

"We should."

"I'm going to ride with the ladies."

He stared at her another moment before almost hesitantly nodding. "Of course. I'll see you at the dinner."

Before Thaddeus could argue with her, she scurried away, desperate to put space between her and this man who seemed to turn her heart to putty.

CHAPTER FORTY-TWO

MIRANDA SPENT the rehearsal dinner trying to avoid Thaddeus.

She wasn't sure why she'd ever thought something between them could work. If she were wise, she'd keep her distance.

But her heart tugged at the thought of never seeing him again.

She was quite the mess, wasn't she?

To be fair, the whole issue with Mars still had her shaken.

She couldn't believe that man had shown up here. At first, she'd thought Brian had been the one behind everything. But he wasn't. He'd been far away all this time. All along, it had been Mars. She never would've guessed this had anything to do with her career.

She'd never thought of it as dangerous.

Miranda knew she was still in jeopardy. Clearly, something else was going on too, and she couldn't wait to hear an update. Had any new clues been found in the motel? Did Grant have any leads as to who might have killed the man they'd found?

So much was still unresolved.

Including what was happening between her and Thaddeus.

She glanced across the room at him as he laughed with Grant about something. Miranda had to admit that Mars' words had gotten to her some. She tried not to let them.

But, for a long time, she'd felt like the outsider Mars said she was. The nobody. The invisible one.

She'd worked hard to correct that, but, in the process, she had lost herself.

How could she fix that?

A surge of determination rushed through her.

She wasn't defined by her job or her looks. Those things didn't make her who she was. Neither did a man and his acceptance or rejection.

God had been teaching her that her worth was found in Him alone.

Now it was time to start living like it.

———

THADDEUS HAD THOUGHT about his kiss with Miranda all night.

And about how quickly things had gone south afterward.

He'd thought so much about it that he couldn't sleep and instead tossed and turned in bed.

He wanted to deny that Miranda's statement about him continuing to make assumptions concerning her was correct. But he couldn't do that.

Because she was absolutely right.

He wasn't sure how to fix things between him and Miranda. Or if it was even possible. But he had to try.

At least Mars Jenson was behind bars.

The man had clearly been trying to rattle Miranda by bringing up aspects of her past she might find disconcerting. Apparently, it had worked. She'd looked as if Mars had slapped her in the face as he'd said the cruel words.

Thaddeus had wanted to pummel the guy for it.

It didn't matter to him how Miranda had looked in the past. He liked her for the person he'd met on that date, the one who hadn't been putting on airs. She'd been the woman with the easy smile and the friendly laugh who wasn't afraid to get dirty.

In fact, that was the woman he'd spent the last several days with. Throughout it all, she'd been down-to-earth, vulnerable, yet tough at the same time.

That was the woman he wanted.

In fact, that was the woman Miranda was, no matter what she looked like.

Even if she did go back to pretending she was a perfect fit for the fast-paced New York career scene, her inner core would be the same. She would still have the same fears, vulnerability, and strengths.

If Thaddeus had met her for the first time in New York, if he'd dated her there, he would have seen right through to her core just the same.

He never should have doubted her. Instead, he'd added insult to injury by asking which Miranda he would be getting if they were together.

He couldn't blame her for getting upset with him.

But none of that mattered now. Tomorrow, he would leave to go back to Texas. He had to make some decisions about his future. Get his life and his career heading in a direction he could live with.

Finally, he climbed out of bed. He'd get a cup of coffee and return to his room. He'd keep the lights out and be as quiet as possible in hopes not to wake anyone else.

When he glanced at the clock beside his bed, he saw it was only 4:30 a.m.

As soon as he stepped into the kitchen, he saw Grant sitting at the dinette there, already sipping a fresh cup of java.

"Morning," Grant said, sounding entirely too perky for this time of day.

"Morning." Thaddeus grabbed his own cup and inhaled the bitter scent before sitting down across from his friend. "You're up early."

"Couldn't sleep. Too much on my mind."

"Are you ready for the big day?"

"More than ready." His voice sounded upbeat as he took another sip of his coffee.

"No doubts?"

"Not a single one." Grant grinned, his eyes beaming with joy. "I feel like the luckiest guy in the whole world right now."

A moment of envy shot through Thaddeus. That was what he wanted for his own life also.

Had he ruined his one chance at finding true love with the woman of his dreams?

He still wasn't sure.

"I'm really happy for you," Thaddeus finally said.

"Thanks, man. I'm glad you could come out here to be a part of this with me."

"You know I wouldn't miss it." Thaddeus shifted. "I know you don't want to think about anything but your wedding right now, but I've been anxious to hear if you guys found anything down in that motel."

"We've collected some evidence—to check DNA. But, of course, we'll need something to compare it to. But I think your theory is right about the bank robberies. It really does make sense, as does Bobby Joe's involvement."

"That was all Miranda. She's the one who put that together."

Grant's gaze locked on his. "She's quite the woman, isn't she?"

"Yes, she is." Thaddeus quickly shoved those thoughts away. He'd really blown it last night, and he was anxious to fix things between them.

But he knew some things weren't fixable. Would that be the case for their relationship?

Grant continued, "Anyway, we think three men were working together and using the motel as their home base to hide the money and their plans. But what I'm not quite sure about is what that guy meant when he shot up this place and told you guys to give back what you took."

Thaddeus leaned back and let out a deep breath. "That's something we haven't figured out yet. Do you think they would follow Miranda back to New York over this thing they want?"

"That's a great question, and I'm not sure of the answer. Let's just hope that we can figure out who is behind this, resolve it, and move on." Grant sounded exhausted, as if the past week had taken a toll on him.

That was all Thaddeus wanted also. To move on.

But how could he if Miranda might still be in danger?

He'd never intended to stumble onto this crime.

More than anything, all he wanted was to fix things with Miranda and keep her safe. Only then could he concentrate on going home and figuring out what to do next.

CHAPTER FORTY-THREE

MIRANDA AWOKE when she heard movement in her room.

Had she overslept?

She blinked open her eyes. The room was still dark. As she glanced to the side, she saw the curtains by the balcony door blowing in the wind.

What? She hadn't left that open. She was sure of it.

She started to sit up.

Before she could, a masked man leaned over her bed.

She tried to scramble back. But the man pulled a gun out and held it to her temple. "Scream, and I'll put a bullet through your head."

Miranda had no doubt that he meant it.

"Where is it?" he demanded. "Speak quietly."

Her mind was still fuzzy with confusion. It took her a moment to realize what he might be talking about. Then she remembered. "I already gave the papers to the police. It's too late."

"No, I mean the pen."

"The pen? What pen?"

"The pen you took from the box. It was in there with the papers."

"What does that have to do with any of this?"

"It doesn't matter. I just need it."

"It's on my dresser," she said.

"You're going to go get it, and, if you make one wrong move, I'll use this gun. Do you understand?"

"Okay," she murmured. "Okay."

Miranda knew better than to make a wrong move. Based on the hard look in this man's eyes he was telling the truth.

Why did those eyes look familiar? Where had she seen this man before?

She'd have to figure that out later. With trembling legs, she stood and walked to the dresser, the man shadowing her every step.

She felt around for the pen in the dark. She flinched when she knocked over a bottle of lotion.

"Quiet," the man snarled and shoved the gun harder against her temple.

Taking in a deep breath, she continued. Her fingers grazed the pen.

She handed it to him. "Here. Take it. I don't even know why you want it."

With the gun still pointed at her, he took the pen and unscrewed the cylinder. He pulled out a piece of paper hidden inside.

Miranda sucked in a breath. "What's that?"

"Just some codes that help us get through the security systems," he muttered. "I stuck them in here for safekeeping, and, unless we have these, we can't do any more jobs."

Of all the places to hide something like that. She never would have thought a pen would hold such information. The everyday item seemed insignificant, so much so that she'd almost forgotten she even had it. And, as such, she'd never thought of turning the pen over to Grant or anyone else working the case.

But there was nothing she could do about that now.

"I see." She prayed that he would leave now that he had the information he wanted.

Please, God . . .

Instead, the man tugged her arm, pulling her toward the balcony. "You're coming with me."

Fear flooded Miranda as survival instinct kicked in. "You have what you want. You can let me go."

"It's not that easy. I need leverage."

If Miranda knew anything, she knew that she couldn't go with this man. But how was she going to get out of this without getting herself—or anyone else in this house—killed?

———

THADDEUS NEEDED to talk to Miranda. That was all there was to it. No more dancing around the issues between them.

He knew it was too early now. But as he passed her door on the way back to his room, he heard a whisper coming from inside.

Was she talking on the phone?

Or was somebody in there with her?

It almost sounded like . . . a man.

Alarm raced through Thaddeus. What if one of the people involved with these bank robberies had somehow snuck inside?

His thoughts raced back to the conversation he'd

just had with Grant. Someone still wanted something from them.

Had someone scaled the tree again in order to get onto the balcony? To get to Miranda?

Surely, Miranda had left her door locked.

But maybe someone had found a way to unlock it.

At this point, Thaddeus couldn't be certain of anything.

He pressed his ear to the door, not wanting to make any moves that might get her hurt.

As soon as he heard the words, *I need leverage*, Thaddeus knew he had to step in.

Now.

He only wished he had time to alert Grant and grab his gun, but he didn't.

Instead, he threw the door open and froze as the light from the hallway illuminated a masked man holding a gun to Miranda's head.

His heart pounded in his ears as the direness of the situation hit him.

"You don't want to do that." Thaddeus didn't bother to keep his voice low.

Hopefully, Grant would hear what was going on and could come help.

"Stay back or I'll kill her." The man pressed the gun harder into Miranda's temple until she yelped.

The sight of Miranda looking so vulnerable made Thaddeus' heart twist.

He couldn't let things end this way. He had to help her.

Whatever it took.

"Don't take her," Thaddeus told the man. "Take me."

The man let out a gruff laugh. "I've got to say she's a lot easier to handle than you would be. If you know what's best, you're going to step back and get out of my way right now."

"I can't do that," Thaddeus said. "I can't let you take her from here."

"I either take her or I kill you and then take her. You pick."

Thaddeus glanced at the patio and saw movement.

Grant. Had he somehow crossed from an adjoining balcony onto Miranda's?

Thaddeus needed to stall long enough for Grant to get a good shot.

There was only one way he could think of to distract this guy.

Thaddeus swallowed hard before raising his

hands. "How about this? We just let you walk away. We don't make a big deal of this. Whatever is going on isn't worth someone being killed. Take your money. Rob your banks. Just don't kill anybody else."

The man's eyes narrowed. "You don't know what you're talking about. I haven't killed anyone. Yet."

"We know you killed Bobby Joe."

"That wasn't me!" His voice rose. "I had nothing to do with that."

"Then who did?"

The man shook his head. "It doesn't matter."

Thaddeus glanced at Grant again, trying not to clue this man in as to what was going on. But Thaddeus knew that his friend didn't have a good shot yet. Not from the angle where they were standing. It was too risky.

But this guy seemed to be coming more unhinged by the moment.

They would need to act soon before Miranda became another victim.

If he could just get the guy to move toward the patio, Grant would have a better chance of getting a good shot.

"You're not making the situation any better by taking Miranda with you." Thaddeus kept his voice steady and controlled, like that of a negotiator. "Just push her to me and you can run out on the balcony. And nobody else will know what's happening."

"I'm not stupid. You'll come right after me." His finger twitched on the trigger.

Fear burned a searing path to Thaddeus' heart.

He couldn't let this happen.

The only way he knew to stop this might just make him lose any chance he might have with Miranda.

But saving her life would be worth any sacrifice he could make. Even if it meant she might not ever forgive him.

CHAPTER FORTY-FOUR

AS MIRANDA FELT the gun press into her temple, her fear only intensified.

This man was going to kill her. Maybe not here. Maybe not now.

But this story was going to end with her death.

Nausea churned inside her at the thought.

"You should just walk away," the man told Thaddeus. "That's how you can really help this situation."

Her heart pounded harder.

What if Thaddeus did just like he suggested? What if he left her here, just like Brian had left her in that store? Just like her dad had left her when she needed him as a child?

Her throat seemed to swell.

But Thaddeus wasn't like that . . . was he? Could

Miranda really depend on anybody to be there for her? Or did she only have herself and God?

Thaddeus didn't say anything for a moment.

The man shifted, exposing the watch he wore on his wrist.

That's when she realized who he was.

Miranda had seen him before. Even talked to him.

But was it even possible she might be able to get through to him?

She didn't know the answer to that for sure.

"You know what?" Thaddeus held up his hands and took a step back. "I came here to be in a wedding. I didn't ask for any of this."

Miranda's stomach plunged to the floor. This couldn't be happening.

Not again.

Not Thaddeus.

"I'm out of here." He took another step back.

His gaze met hers, something unspoken and pleading in his eyes.

What was he trying to tell her? That he was sorry, but she wasn't worth the trouble? That he was leaving her like the other men in her life had?

Or was it something else? Something deeper. More meaningful.

As she stared into his eyes, something shifted inside her. A sense of peace came over her. And she knew.

She *knew* this man would never abandon her.

He hadn't left her in the motel, buried beneath tons of sand. He hadn't left her to deal with all this on her own. And he wasn't going to leave her now.

As the man with the gun tugged her toward the balcony, Thaddeus gave her a slight nod.

And she allowed the man to start dragging her away.

That's when a gunshot blasted through the air.

THADDEUS HELD his breath as he waited to see who'd fired.

The next instant, the masked man crumpled to the floor.

As he did, Thaddeus lunged forward, grabbed Miranda, and pulled her out of the way. He kicked the man's gun out of reach.

Miranda melted into his arms. As she did, Grant stormed into the room and knelt beside the gunman, handcuffs in hand.

He'd shot the man's shoulder, and blood poured

from the wound. But it wasn't a fatal hit. The man would live to suffer the consequences of his actions.

As Grant pulled off the mask, a familiar face appeared.

"Stephen, the pool guy," Miranda muttered. "I recognized your waterproof watch."

"You've been behind this?" Thaddeus demanded.

Stephen's gaze darkened. "I have bills to pay. What can I say?"

"You can say a lot. In fact, you have *a lot* of explaining to do." Grant pulled him to his feet despite the man's protests. As he did that, Thaddeus grabbed his phone and called in an ambulance.

"How did you find that old motel to begin with?" Grant demanded.

"Why's that matter?"

"Because I asked." Grant's voice left no room for argument.

"You shot me. I need medical attention."

"An ambulance is on the way. Start talking. Now."

Behind him, Thaddeus could hear people gathering near the door.

Abigail appeared and ushered them away before any of her bridesmaids saw the scene inside the room.

Stephen let out a sigh. "My friends and I were messing around in the woods. It was after a storm, and one of the doors to the old Sand Spur became uncovered. We decided to explore, and that's when we realized how perfect that place would be if we needed somewhere to lie low. But when we came back again the next day, the door was gone."

Grant continued to stare at him. "That seems to be a theme."

"Anyway, Carl and I—" Stephen clamped his mouth down as if he hadn't meant to say the name.

"Carl Laski, the handyman?" Grant's voice pitched with surprise. "The one who was just over here patching up bullet holes?"

Stephen rolled his eyes. "Whatever. It's not like you're not going to find out anyway. But, yeah, the two of us were in on it. We were determined to figure out a way to access that door again, and we eventually did."

"How?" Thaddeus asked.

"Since Carl knows about construction, he put together that scaffolding to make sure it was safe for us to come and go. We planned it so the entry would be hidden by some of the brush from Wash Woods. It was really perfect until . . ." His gaze fell on

Miranda. "Until she got too close to our secret entrance."

"You're the one who hit me over the head when I was on the sand dune," Miranda muttered.

Stephen shrugged. "I was just trying to scare you away. I never thought it would turn into this. Then you fell into the motel and found Bobby Joe. Talk about bad timing."

"I'm going to get back to that dead body in a minute," Grant muttered. "Were you the one who shot at Thaddeus and me when we were on the dune?"

"I was over here working on the hot tub." Stephen smirked. "That was Carl. He's not the brightest guy, but he's got guts. He's the one who really pushed us to do this."

"Even after you did all that and tried to scare Miranda and Thaddeus away, why did you keep coming after them? What was it you wanted so badly?"

"He wanted a pen I picked up in the motel," Miranda spoke up.

"All this is over a pen?" Grant asked. "An ink pen?"

"A fountain pen, to be exact. The pen has a list of codes inside so Carl and I can get past the security systems at various banks," he boasted as if proud of his ingenious hiding place.

Thaddeus had to admit, he'd never encountered such a scheme before.

"Bobby Joe gave us that information in exchange for our silence about some other less-than-upright deeds that he was involved with."

"So that's what this has been about the whole time?" Thaddeus shook his head as if disgusted. "You were just trying to get that fountain pen back?"

"I figured one of you had found it along with the papers that were missing. When I came here to look for it, you two were already back from wherever you'd gone. When I knew you had seen me outside the front door, I knew I couldn't let you find out who I was. I started shooting. Besides, I figured if I could scare you guys away maybe I had a chance to get inside and look for it. But it still didn't work. Nothing worked."

"Why did you kill Bobby Joe?" Thaddeus asked.

He hesitated as if reluctant to admit his part in this. "It wasn't me."

Grant nudged him. "Keep talking."

"Okay. Fine. He wanted out. That's when Carl pulled the trigger. I didn't want anything to do with that part of the deal. I just need the money." His voice rose as if panic was setting in.

Thaddeus stepped closer, his gaze narrowed. "What do you need the money so badly for?"

"I've made too many of the wrong people mad. As soon as I have enough cash, I'm getting out of town. I'm going to start fresh away from this place."

"Who did you make mad? Drug dealers?"

His face clouded. "Maybe."

"You'd rather run than pay them what you owe them," Thaddeus continued. "Even though you know they will try to find you. Not too bright if you ask me."

"Yeah, well. Nobody asked you."

Instead of responding, Thaddeus tugged Miranda to him. Hoping—praying—she would understand his actions.

Sirens sounded out front.

Backup was here.

Maybe this was finally over.

CHAPTER FORTY-FIVE

MIRANDA STARED at herself in the mirror again before nodding, satisfied with what she saw.

It was time for this show to get on the road.

The wedding was supposed to start in thirty minutes.

The last twenty-four hours had been a whirlwind. Stephen had been arrested. Carl had been tracked down and also arrested. People had been updated and reassured.

Then the wedding party had gotten ready and had been escorted to the church.

She and Thaddeus still hadn't had the opportunity to talk.

But she felt like they had so much to say to each other.

As the wedding coordinator stepped in the room, a noise caught her ear.

Rain.

It pounded on the church roof.

"They say it's good luck," Miranda told Abigail. "Right?"

Abigail touched her veil and nodded. "Either way, I'm not superstitious. I'm just ready to do this."

"You make a beautiful bride." Miranda meant the words. Her friend was stunning.

"Thank you. You look wonderful also." As the rest of the bridesmaids scurried from the room, Abigail grabbed her arm, holding her in place. "By the way, Grant and I may have asked you to come here early in hopes you and Thaddeus would pick up where you left off."

Miranda raised an eyebrow. "I figured that much."

"It's just that the two of you looked so happy in Austin."

"We were."

"Is there any chance now?" She looked at Miranda hopefully.

"I haven't exactly talked to Thaddeus about it, but I think there might be."

A grin spread across Abigail's face. "That would be an awesome wedding present, by the way."

Miranda laughed. "I'll keep that in mind. But do I need to remind you that today is about you?"

She clutched her bouquet and let out a breath. "You're right. This is one of the best days of my life, and I'm so glad my best friend can spend it with me."

The two hugged.

Before they could talk any longer, the coordinator motioned to them, anxious to have everyone in place.

Arm in arm, they stepped into the foyer and waited for their turn to march down the aisle.

THADDEUS STOOD beside Grant on the stage, his eyes fastened to the door at the end of the aisle as the bridesmaids started down.

When he saw Miranda, his breath caught.

She was a brunette again.

When had that happened?

Miranda's gaze caught his, and she smiled, almost as if she'd wanted to see his reaction.

He liked the change—but he liked Miranda

whatever her hair color. Whatever she wore. Whatever direction she took her career. Wherever she chose to live.

Although Thaddeus had zoned out a time or two —his gaze and thoughts remained on Miranda and the conversation they needed to have—the ceremony was beautiful.

It wasn't until afterward as everyone gathered at the reception that he had the chance to talk to her alone.

The reception was at a place called Smith's Hope, an old barn that had been converted into a celebration space.

A live band played in the corner, and people danced in the center. A nice spread of food— including Hillsdale's famous barbecue and Mrs. Minnie's crab cakes—were against another wall. Haybales formed seating areas and string lights stretched across the rafters.

Rain pounded the tin roof above them, only adding to the romantic atmosphere.

Thaddeus cut through the crowd until he found Miranda. As she looked away from her conversation with some other bridesmaids, her eyes brightened when she saw him.

"Hi." She grinned.

"Hi." He shoved his hands in his pockets. "You look nice. I like your hair."

She touched a curl. "I decided it was time for a change. When your life flashes before your eyes, some of those details become clearer."

"Yes, they do."

"I actually called my editor today. Even though it's a Saturday, she was at work."

"And?"

"I quit."

His eyes widened. "You quit? Just like that?"

Miranda nodded. "I did. And I feel like I lost about thirty pounds in the process. I didn't realize how much that job was stressing me out."

"Good for you. What are you going to do now?"

She shrugged and glanced toward the ceiling in thought. "That's a good question. I'm not exactly sure yet. But I'm thinking about freelancing for a while. I think I've made enough contacts to have a good shot at it. And, I have a really good story going with this whole hotel fiasco."

"I think you'll be wildly successful with anything you choose to do."

The two of them stared at each other another moment, something unseen seeming to swirl between them.

As the band started a new song, Miranda took his hand. "We have to dance."

He let out a chuckle at her eagerness. "I'd love to."

But instead of pulling him onto the dance floor, she pulled him outside . . . in the rain.

As the first verse started and he recognized "Brown Eyed Girl," everything made sense. "Just like our date," he murmured.

"Just like our date."

He wrapped his arms around her waist as she put her arms around his neck. As rain poured down on them, they began swaying to the music.

"Does this mean you forgive me?" Thaddeus held his breath. Her answer—this moment—could determine the course of his life.

"For . . . ?"

"I would never abandon you, Miranda. Please know that."

"Ah, you must be referring to the little stunt you played this morning. Pretending to step away and leave me with a gunman."

"You knew I was pretending?"

"Yep." She nodded.

"How did you know?"

"When I looked into your eyes, I felt it. I think

maybe God allowed that moment in my life to show me that not only would He never leave me, but that He brought a man into my life that would stand by my side no matter what."

Thaddeus' hopes soared. But there was one more thing he needed to address. "I was thinking about our conversation, well, our fight that we had. And you were right. I was still making assumptions. I realize now that no matter what you look like, how you dress, or where you work or live, there is only one you. I want *you* in my life, Miranda."

"That's good to know, because I want you in my life also." After a moment she added, "We both made assumptions that almost kept us apart. And I'm sorry too. So where does this leave us?"

The sounds of the reception faded into the background. Everyone was near yet no one was close. The rain gave them their own private moment.

"Levi offered me a job here in Cape Corral," he told her quietly.

She jerked her gaze up to meet his. "What? That's great. What did you say?"

"I said I'll seriously consider it."

"That would mean you have to move here."

"It does." He nodded slowly.

"I was actually thinking about relocating here also."

Thaddeus raised his eyebrows. "Is that right? I think that would make Abigail and Grant very happy."

"That would make me very happy also . . . especially if you were here with me."

Wasting no more time, he leaned forward and pressed his lips against hers.

He hoped to do this for a long time . . . maybe even for the rest of his life.

~~~

If you enjoyed this book, please consider leaving a review!

ALSO BY CHRISTY BARRITT:

SALTWATER COWBOYS

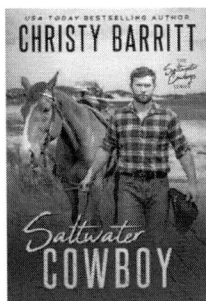

Saltwater Cowboy

He's trying to forget. She'd give anything to remember.

Officer Levi Sutherland wants to protect the wild horses of Cape Corral and keep the island residents safe. But memories of his deceased wife haunt him at every turn and make him long for a fresh start. When a woman washes ashore with a bullet wound and no memories, Levi knows he can't leave until he discovers what happened to her.

The woman—whose necklace reads Dani— captures Levi's attention like no one has in a long time. But which side of the law is she on? Could

Dani be mixed up with other mysterious incidents happening on the island?

Together, can the two find answers and create new memories? Or will secrets tear them apart and destroy a future as uncertain as Dani's past?

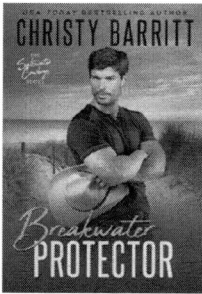

Breakwater Protector

One secret will tear them apart. The other will pull them closer.

Lizzie McCreary needs to disappear. As danger stalks her, she escapes to windswept Cape Corral with her eight-year-old son, Preston. The isolated island offers her a desperate hope for safety.

Saltwater cowboy Dash Fulton isn't looking for love. Yet when he rescues a woman and boy from the woods, he immediately feels a bond with the two. He can sense the pair are harboring secrets. The question is, what are they?

Dash has secrets of his own, and pressure continues to mount for him to come clean. But as he's caught up in the peril surrounding Lizzie and Preston, his own problems become a low priority. He can't let anyone hurt the sweet single mom and her precocious son.

As more details come to light, will wounds from the past ultimately drive Lizzie and Dash apart? Or will the man chasing Lizzie destroy any hope for the future?

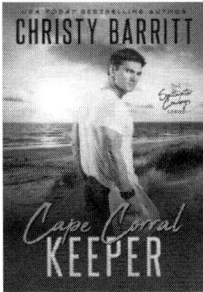

Cape Corral Keeper

They agreed to marry. But they never agreed to fall in love.

When Cape Corral Fire Chief Dillon McGrath saves a woman wearing a wedding dress from drowning, he knows he'll have a great story to tell the guys at the station later. He never expected to get personally involved in the woman's plight to stay alive.

Gracie Loveland had no choice but to run only moments before saying "I do" to her manipulative fiancé. Staying would have ultimately meant her death at the hands of the cruel man. Desperation, along with a dormant feistiness, surfaces as she fights to survive.

Only one plan might keep Gracie safe and help Dillon preserve the island's wild horses. The idea seems crazy, but Dillon and Gracie can think of no other options. However, a foe from Gracie's past is closing in, determined to get what he wants regardless of whose life he destroys in the process.

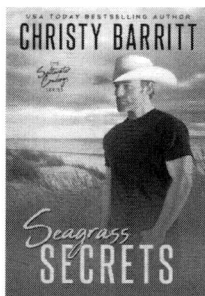

Seagrass Secrets

He's her best friend. She's the woman of his dreams.

Firefighter Colby Morris needs answers. After discovering a dead body, he then learns his best friend's address was in the man's pocket. He'll do anything to keep Emmy safe —yet he wants to keep his heart safe also. That's why he's never told Emmy he's in love with her.

Emmy Sutherland is trying to make amends after she hits a man with her truck while driving in a torrential downpour. When the island's clinic floods, she has no choice but to let the stranger stay at her inn. But recent events on Cape Corral have her feeling apprehensive.

Events continue to escalate, leaving Colby and Emmy scrambling to find answers. But as more secrets are uncovered, more danger arises. Can Colby and Emmy discover the truth? Or will their feelings get in the way—endangering not only their lives but their lifelong friendship?

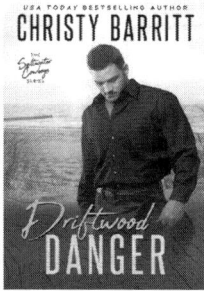

Driftwood Danger

He's on one side of the fight to preserve Cape Corral. She's on the other.

Abigail Ferguson wakes up in a strange place with bruises on her face and her hands bound. Someone is trying to teach her family a painful lesson and using Abigail as a pawn. When she's able to call for help, only one person comes to mind—law enforcement officer Grant Matthews.

Grant has been crazy about Abigail since they met. But her wealthy family is a long-standing enemy of locals, and dating her would feel like a betrayal to the community he serves. However, when Abigail is abducted and needs his help, nothing will stop him from rescuing and protecting her.

As Abigail's captor makes it clear he has more dastardly deeds planned, Grant and Abigail work together to try to find answers. But their growing feelings—and the obstacles between them—might put Abigail in even more danger. Can the two figure out this man's identity before it's too late? Or will the clever madman taunting Abigail stop at nothing to achieve what he wants?

ABOUT THE AUTHOR

USA Today has called Christy Barritt's books "scary, funny, passionate, and quirky."

Christy writes both mystery and romantic suspense novels that are clean with underlying messages of faith. Her books have won the Daphne du Maurier Award for Excellence in Suspense and Mystery, have been twice nominated for the Romantic Times Reviewers' Choice Award, and have finaled for both a Carol Award and Foreword Magazine's Book of the Year.

She is married to her Prince Charming, a man who thinks she's hilarious—but only when she's not trying to be. Christy is a self-proclaimed klutz, an avid music lover who's known for spontaneously bursting into song, and a road trip aficionado.

When she's not working or spending time with her family, she enjoys singing, playing the guitar, and exploring small, unsuspecting towns where people have no idea how accident-prone she is.

Find Christy online at:
www.christybarritt.com
www.facebook.com/christybarritt
www.twitter.com/cbarritt

Sign up for Christy's newsletter to get information on all of her latest releases here: **www.christybarritt.com/newsletter-sign-up/**

If you enjoyed this book, please consider leaving a review.

Made in the USA
Middletown, DE
23 May 2024

54752160R00222